DEWEY FAIRCHILD,
PARENT PROBLEM SOLVER

Lorri Horn

Amberjack Publishing
New York, New York

Amberjack Publishing
228 Park Avenue S #89611
New York, NY 10003-1502
http://amberjackpublishing.com

Publisher's Cataloging-in-Publication data
Names: Horn, Lorri, author.
Title: Dewey Fairchild , parent problem solver / Lorri Horn.
Description: New York, NY : Amberjack Pub., 2017.
Identifiers: 9781944995164 (hardcover) | 9781944995331 (ebk.) | LCCN 2016962763
Summary: Dewey Fairchild can solve any problem parents might cause their children. But what will Dewey do when the parents that are causing problems are his own?
Subjects: LCSH Parent and child--Juvenile fiction. | Self-actualization (Psychology)--Fiction. | Parenting--Juvenile fiction. | BISAC JUVENILE FICTION / Family / General
Classification: LCC PZ7 .H7888 De 2017 | DDC [Fic]--dc23

Cover Design & Illustrations: Agnieszka Grochalska

To Brian and Florian

Showering 101

Having too many secrets is never a good idea, but Dewey Fairchild really, *really* hated that his mom made him bathe *every* day. It was a waste of time. It was a waste of water.

As the bathroom filled up with steam, he sat on the toilet lid in his underwear and socks flipping through an old *Lego* magazine.

"Dewey, make sure you wash your hair!" his mother called out through the closed bathroom door. His smooth camel brown hair hung below his ears. His eyes, seemingly undecided on one

1

color, were a blended hazel with a honeydew hue.

"OK," he called back to her.

Ergh. Now he had to dunk his head in the sink. Still it was better than getting all wet, so he stuck his head quickly under the faucet for a quick soak.

"Ouch!" he cried, but forced himself to stifle the sound, so his mother wouldn't hear. "Stupid faucet," he grumbled.

The pages of his magazine started to get floppy from the steam, so he abandoned it in favor of drawing stick figures and figure eights in the bathroom mirror.

Finally, when a respectable amount of time had passed for faking a shower, Dewey leaned in and turned off the running water, trying not to get his arm or the floor wet.

Just then, a couple quick knocks and the handle on the door knob turned. A quick wave of shock shot into his fingertips and tingled up his scalp—there he stood, in his underwear and socks, totally dry except for some damp hair with a shower curtain in his hand!

No. Wait. He had locked the door. It turned but didn't open.

"Want me to hand you your towel?" his mom asked through the door. "Dewey, I won't come in without knocking, but I really don't want you to lock the door."

"OK. Sorry. No, I got it," replied Dewey, hiding himself behind the shower curtain, as if she could somehow see him through the door.

Dewey's heart rate slowed back down after his narrow escape. He put on his fresh clothes quickly. His assistant, Clara, had contacted him earlier and said that Danny Tedphrey had requested his services. He wanted to get back up to the office, ASAP.

How It All Began

One of Dewey's favorite new computer games involved simply clicking for cookies. The more you clicked, the more cookies you collected.

"Arrrgh! My arm is burning! I'm up to 8,000 cookies," yelled out Dewey's friend Colin while they each clicked away one day in the computer lab during lunch. "I'm going to get carpet tunnel!! But I don't care! Must. Get. 9,000!"

"Shh! Carpal tunnel, you goof. You need to buy more grandmas and farms, so they can make cookies for you."

"What I need is a little brother or one of those Harry Potter house elves I can command to click for me."

"Ha! Oh! I'm at 12,000!" Dewey announced.

Colin Decker stood about fifty-four inches tall, with brown eyes, brown skin, and curly black hair. That made him half an inch taller than Dewey, three-and-a-half times the height of a bowling pin, seven-tenths the height of Michael Jordan, one-fifth the height of a giraffe, one-sixteenth the height of a giant sequoia tree, one-seventeenth the height of the Statue of Liberty, and about 10,000 times the height of a sheet of paper.

Or so Colin had read online. You can't believe everything you read, though. So one of these days, before he grew too much, he planned on testing some of these out.

"Holy narwhal! My grandmas are losing their teeth."

Dewey laughed. Colin was obsessed with narwhals, those great whales of the arctic whose males grew up to sixteen feet long and had a single, gigantic tusk, like a unicorn, up to ten feet in length.

Grandmas, on the other hand, needed steel plated rolling pins to stand up to the great forces of nature. Or so it seemed.

This was the scene when their other lunch pal, Seraphina, shared a problem, and Dewey really had nothing better to do than help her (they really weren't supposed to be playing games in the lab). Plus, she always had good snacks, and he always felt hungry.

"I just can't take one more single day of it. My mother is a complete nut job. You *have* to help me!"

Seraphina Johnson was definitely flipping out. She came right at him, her books piled up under her lunch tray, the cheese sliding off of her pizza boat as her tray took a shortcut down her science book, and the juice from her fruit cup sloshed all over her fries.

"Um, watch your lunch!" Dewey cried as the tray slid off, narrowly missing the computer table and falling right into his hands. He wiggled the cheese back into place and balanced the tray on his knee.

"What!?" he asked, sucking the grease off of his fingers as Seraphina shot him a look for poking at her cheese. She grabbed her lunch back, and they all headed out to the lunch tables.

"She's insane, that's what. Do you know that she still holds my hand when we cross the street?! When we got to school today, she actually parked the car, walked me in, and held my hand until we got to the other side." Seraphina moved her hair out of her face, sat down, and stared at them for a reply.

Dewey and Colin sat across from her at the tables, and Dewey took a bite of his peanut butter and jelly sandwich. There was just nothing about a school lunch that looked appetizing to him. Too much sauce on the pizza. Too much cheese.

Seraphina didn't seem to be enjoying it much either as she went on and on about her mother. At least she hadn't taken a bite. Nothing not to like about the fries though; he reached over and grabbed a few that seemed to have escaped the puddle of fruit slosh.

Dewey's mom had made his sandwich. He knew because it was cut in triangles, not in half, which was his dad's style. He liked triangles better—much more satisfying biting into the corners. And what's up with the crust anyway? Why wouldn't his parents cut it off? It couldn't be healthier to eat the crust just because it's darker, right? Were there more minerals or vitamins in the crust? It didn't make any sense.

"Are you listening to me?!" Seraphina let go of her long, brown, curly hair, which she'd been twisting while carrying on about her mother's overprotective ways. He was pretty sure he'd caught *most* of what she'd said.

Chips or pretzels were a must with PBJ,

because the salt mixed with the sweetness of the jelly was epic. He wanted to say so but didn't want to seem insensitive to the plight of his fellow parent-sufferer.

"Maybe I can help," he said, pushing a chip and then a french fry into his mouth. "Let me follow you guys around a bit when your mom doesn't know and see if I can figure out what the fruit is going on."

Fruit. That had reminded him. He had a juicy nectarine in his lunch sack.

Colin, who had been mostly bored by the theatrics and lost in his own thoughts, looked up from his lunch. "Wait, what?" he said. Now *this* was going to be interesting.

"Come in. My mom is still sleeping," Seraphina whispered sleepily as she opened the door and shoved a bite-sized doggie treat in Bigboy's mouth so he wouldn't bark. Bigboy was a Miniature

Teacup Poodle.

They had it all planned out. Dewey would remain hidden and follow them for an entire day to gather data on the world's most overprotective mom. Then they'd plot out how to hinder her humiliating ways before they completely unhinged Seraphina.

"Here." Seraphina jammed a Ziplock bag full of doggie treats into Dewey's hand. "Once Bigboy knows you're here, we should be fine . . . but if he seems restless or too interested, just give him one of these. He's a sucker for a treat."

"Me, too," said Dewey. "Did you figure out how to feed me while we're at it?"

"Yes. I've got food and water stations set up for you at the various posts. As long as you don't sneeze or choke or something until she goes upstairs or to work, we should be good."

"Where do you guys start your day together? Kitchen or bedroom?"

"I'd say mostly the kitchen. She'll call me

down to breakfast. You can meet us there. Station one is behind the curtains, so that's perfect!"

Seraphina's mom began her morning in the usual way. The alarm went off at 5:40 a.m. She snoozed it once, but not before trying to rouse Seraphina's dad who mumbled, "Um hmm."

Ten minutes later, the news came on again; she felt for the off button, kicked the lightweight down covers off of herself, and got out of bed.

"Dear, it's time to get up," she said, her own voice rising with each of the words as she spoke them. She headed off to check her morning emails and shower before making breakfast and sending her family on their way.

When she came down to the table, Dewey felt more nervous than he'd anticipated.

Um, he thought to himself, *this was kind of a dumb idea.* He could hear his own breath behind the curtains and his heart beating in his ears. It thumped fast as she moved around the kitchen, and he pictured her eyes landing on his socked feet behind the curtains or the small protrusion that was his body.

She didn't notice Dewey though. What she did notice was that her husband was still upstairs with evidently no signs of human life coming from up there. She sighed. "Go wake up your father, Seraphina."

Seraphina's mom then began to take out cereal bowls, cut up fruit, and pull out salami, bread, lettuce, carrots, and cookies. If Dewey hadn't known better, he would have thought she had eight arms, not two. He began to relax a little more behind the curtains and leaned against the wall, careful to make sure his feet did not stick out too much.

Seraphina came back down to the table. "He's up," she reported, and began to open a new box of cereal. The plastic seal wouldn't budge though, so Seraphina grabbed her butter knife and attempted to poke a hole in it.

"No, Seraphina! Don't do that. You'll hurt yourself. Come on now! Bring it to me."

Miraculously, a ninth arm appeared; while her mom cut the crust off the sandwich and wrapped it up in a tidy foil square, she tore open the cereal package with her teeth.

Dewey took a bite of a powdered donut and flipped his small notepad out of his pocket to jot down these observations as white powder covered the floor like snow. He rubbed it with his right sock and wrote, *powdered donuts too messy for a stakeout.* Shoving the rest of the donut into his mouth and quietly licking the powder off his fingers, his thoughts wandered . . . it was fascinating. Seraphina's mom cut the crust off the sandwich bread. He jotted that down. It just didn't make sense why his mom wouldn't.

OK, yeah. He'd have to agree it was a waste of food—a *tiny* bit of the edge of food. But was there more to it? Could it really be more nutritious? He had to agree, the darker part looked more nutritious somehow, more like wheat bread than white. And everyone knows wheat bread is better for you. But he'd never heard that about crust, and he was pretty sure his parents hadn't either. Anyway, it made no sense, just because it was on the outside, not in—oops. Seraphina's mom had gone upstairs, and he sort of, kind of, hadn't noticed.

Dewey needed to hide himself in the back of their car for the ride to school. He pulled it off just in time, slipping out through the kitchen door that led to the garage and into the back of the car that Seraphina had left unlocked for him. He tried to close the car door softly, but it didn't close all the way, and he had to pull it harder, which made an unavoidably loud noise. He regretted that he had cut it so close.

As they got into the car, he scrunched up his face in a painful grimace, his heart racing again for the second time today. He thought for sure

Seraphina's mom would ask about the car door noise and discover him, and he held his face in the painful scrunched position as if to somehow ward it off.

"Do you have your lunch?" was all he heard her mother asking. Seraphina affirmed that she did after they had clamored into the car. Dewey, buried under reusable grocery bags and some golf clubs which were already beginning to cut off the circulation in his legs, felt the blood return to his face as the car left the driveway.

"So, how's school, Seraphina?"

"Fine."

"That's great. ¿*Cómo es tu clase de Español?*"

"What? What's that? What are you saying?"

"Come on!"

"It's fine, I guess."

Dewey wanted to bang himself over the head with a golf club for some entertainment.

Then they arrived at school.

Dewey couldn't believe it. Seraphina's mom

looped her arm through Seraphina's and—no, wait, if he wasn't mistaken, she had knotted her arm through Seraphina's in a classic Boy Scout Alpine Butterfly Loop! Just as swiftly, she grabbed Seraphina's hand tightly, as if the butterfly loop wasn't enough! Whoa.

Dewey peered out of the back of the car, fiddling with the extra set of keys that Seraphina had given him. He didn't take his eyes off of her as they got to the corner.

At least she hadn't set the Alpine Knot. That required holding the loop in your *teeth* and pulling both ends with your hands! Still, Seraphina just stood there along with all the other kids with their backpacks, some with wheels, some like camel humps loading them down, but none with the weight that poor Seraphina carried—a nine-and-a-half-year-old with a mother wrapped around her!

When they were out of hearing distance, Dewey climbed out of the back of the car and locked the doors. The alarm gave a little beep, indicating it had been set again. He caught up to the caravan of students and blended in a few steps behind his subjects.

Seraphina's mother clasped her arm while walking all the way across the street and into the building until Seraphina finally wriggled out of her mother's grip to open her locker.

"Would you mind closing your locker door a bit, dear?" her mom asked the kid whose locker was next to Seraphina's.

Seraphina cringed. "Mom!"

"I think you should take your jacket out and bring it with you to class. It gets cold with the air conditioning," her mom added.

Seraphina took it out and threw it over her own face and head.

As if lifting a veil from her pint-sized bride, Seraphina's mom removed the jacket and draped it over her daughter's shoulder, patting her gently as she did.

She walked Seraphina to class and waved goodbye, a four finger flutter through the little glass window in the door.

Pickup time wasn't any better.

Dewey, somewhat exhilarated at the idea of bounding out of class like a superhero trying to get back to Seraphina's mother's car before the two of them did, awaited the final bell.

"Hey, Dewey?" Jack, the kid who sat behind him, was trying to get his attention as the bell rang. Jack's parents actually named him August Jack, but no one ever called him August, except his grandmother whose late father had the same name.

"Not now," said Dewey. "I gotta fly outta here."

"I found out a way to get to the next level on—"

Todd continued talking, but Dewey didn't hear. He was stuffing his books into his bag and throwing it over his shoulder. Just as he was about to head out the door, his teacher, Mrs. Jordan, looked over her shoulder from the whiteboard where she'd been erasing something and said, "Oh, Dewey . . . wait a minute; it's here somewhere." She began to shuffle through papers on her stool, looking for something she wanted to return to him.

Dewey clenched his jaw tightly, willing her to go faster. He was just about to tell her that he could get whatever it was tomorrow, when Todd sidled up, keen to seize the opportunity to finish his thought. "Yeah, so anyway, it's kind of a 'cheat' but all you gotta do is disconnect your internet connection, restart the app, click on the button again . . ."

Now Mrs. Jordan seemed to be waiting for Todd to finish his thought! Dewey wanted to stuff a large sock filled with mud into Todd's mouth, grab the paper that now dangled in her fingers, and just run.

The sea of kids outside the door seemed to be

thinning out. He didn't have much time. *Play. It. Cool,* he told himself. "Thanks, Mrs. Jordan," he replied, gingerly taking the paper from her, and dragging a still-jabbering Todd out the door. Once he hit the hallway, Dewey launched off, calling, "Talk to you later, Todd!" He swiftly navigated his way through the locker line and carpool fleet with his paper flying in his hand like a sail, leaving Todd, with his hands still mid-gesture in explanation, wondering what the heck just happened.

As Dewey approached the parking lot, he stopped running to avoid suspicion. As he tried to catch his breath, he searched around for Seraphina's mom's car. It was there, but at this hour, so was she. Seraphina stood with her, and he could see that she was stalling, having dumped the entire contents of her backpack all over the parking lot. It was a good stalling tactic, but it would have been better if she'd not done so *right* near the back of the car where he needed to get in!

Seraphina stood with her whole body upright against the back of the car like a caught criminal, as her mother didn't want her to get hit by a car passing by. Her mom stooped to pick up pens, sticks of gum, papers, binders, and books, handing them each to Seraphina, who didn't dare leave her stronghold.

As Seraphina and her mother worked to reassemble the backpack, Dewey crept round to the front of the car. "I think there's one under that car there, Mom," directed Seraphina. Dewey took his cue, dashing to the front passenger seat and hopping in. "No, wait. Sorry. I guess I was wrong."

"Seraphina, I think we've got it all."

Seraphina looked over and saw Dewey crouched over in the front seat.

"Yeah, but I can't-get-this-darn-zipper-to-close."

"Careful, Seraphina! That's how you spilled it all before!" her mom shrieked and ran over to help her. She looked down to zip up the back-pack.

At that moment, Dewey rolled his body over the seats into the back of the car, where he settled under the blanket in the back. This time, his heart wasn't racing as much.

Dinnertime at the Johnson's turned into a rated-M video game as Seraphina attempted to use a steak knife.

"Seraphina-a-a-a!" her mom screamed—it was so theatrical that you might have thought the child had put a knife through her mother's heart. "We do not use a steak knife to butter our bread. And furthermore, who gave you a steak knife in the first place?!"

"Well, I'm guessing whoever set the table figured it might be useful, since we're eating steak."

"Don't give me any of your sassafras, Seraphina. You know very well *you* set the table. And Ira, I don't appreciate you smirking," she added to her husband, who couldn't help but smile at the unfolding scene. "Some support here would be greatly appreciated. SHE COULD HAVE JABBED AN ARTERY! SHE COULD HAVE LOST A FINGER!" Mrs. Johnson, hyperventilating with tears in her eyes, could have been heard shrieking at least two houses away.

Dewey found his heart beating a little faster, but this time being caught was the last thing on his mind. Seraphina's mom looked crazed, like some mad-eyed animal. Her hair looked wild and was sticking up like a tumbleweed as her eyes darted back and forth between them. Frankly, Dewey feared for Seraphina and her dad. But they just went right back to eating their dinner. Even Bigboy merely looked up out of one eye then settled back down to his nap.

"Dad, can you pass the butter?" asked Seraphina, and she began to spread it on her bread with her pointer finger. She tore her steak into little pieces with her teeth and set each piece down on her plate.

"Well, that's hardly necessary," Mrs. Johnson objected somewhat resentfully and pouted. It seemed the theatrics were done.

"Oh, sorry. I mean can you *please* pass the butter," corrected Seraphina.

"No, I mean, I'll cut your steak for you, dear. And here's a butter knife. I trust you'll not run off to abuse any cereal bags with it." Seraphina's mom had completely regained her composure and smoothed her hair down with her fingers.

After dinner, Seraphina set off upstairs. As she passed, she gave a little shrug in the direction of Dewey who, feeling less disturbed now, was finishing off a can of sardines. With no signs of Bigboy moving his direction, Dewey comfortably set his sights on dessert—a little chocolate pudding pack. Spoon to mouth, he set his mind to figuring out how to save Seraphina.

Octopushy

Dewey's mother sat across the table from him and moved a little piece of hair out of his eyes. "You look tired," she said to him. "Did you get enough sleep at Clara's?"

Clara Cottonwood was an old (very old, you might say) friend of the family. She had been the birthday girl many (many, many) times, and had the birthday party themes to show for it.

"Let's see," Clara had recounted one day for

Dewey as they sat at her kitchen table, drinking tea and eating her homemade cookies. "In no particular order, there was the princess party, teddy bear party, nail polish party, Minnie Mouse party. I had a ballerina party, a donuts and daisies party, Elmo, pajamas and pancakes, firefighter, buttons and bows, Raggedy Ann party, a sewing one, *Alice in Wonderland, The Wizard of Oz, Pippi Longstocking*—oh, that was a fun time! We all skated over the kitchen floor with buckets of water and scrub brushes attached to our feet! Let's see now, train party, pirates, *Peter Pan*, unicorns, *Howdy Doody*—"

"Howdy Whody?" interrupted Dewey, but Clara just continued right on recalling her birthday party themes as she counted them out on her fingers.

"The polka dot party, my mystery dinner, ice skating, Mother Goose, teen idol, Hawaiian luau, scavenger hunt, tea party, Betty Boop, *Star Wars*, Harry Potter, the petting zoo, a cooking party . . ." She seemed to be slowing her pace down. No. She picked right back up after taking in more air, "A circus party, *Winky Dink and You*, garden party, rainbow party, pony party, jukebox, Justin Bieber, oh, my sweet 16," she paused again to breathe. "Disco, *The Pink Panther*, gay Paris, bowling, Muppets, mermaids, cowboys and Indians—in those days that was done, you know. Pool party, safari, Candyland, *Wonderama*—I got to be Bob McAllister, of course!"

Now she'd lost him again. *Who the heck was Bob McAllister?* He knew from Howdy Whody, though, that there was no point in interrupting her to find out.

"The magic party, the beach party, yes, there was a bug party, Batman, Barbie, Noah's Ark, *Curious George*, a sock hop, picnic party, archae-ological dinosaur bash, purple and pink party, Hot Wheels, spy, spa, twin, *My Little Pony*, cock-tail, construction, reptiles, ice cream social, Lego, country fair, superhero, Angry Birds, post office, rock climbing, casino, science, backwards, movie, puppy, karaoke—ha, that was just a Jukebox redux!" she laughed before continuing. "Art, hats, camping, carousel, puppets, backyard carnival, chocolate party, and go-karts. I think that was all of them. Wonder what we'll do this year, Dewey? Dewey?"

Dewey had felt like crawling in bed and pulling the covers over his head just hearing about all of those parties. At that moment, he didn't think he could possibly come up with another idea if his life depended it on it. Clara, though, had been the guest of honor at all of those parties over the years and still seemed raring to go.

The point is, many years ago, probably somewhere between her Candyland birthday party and her casino one, Clara Cottonwood had been Dewey's dad's babysitter. Eventually, she became an integral part of Dewey's operation. Today, however, she was merely a good neighbor and decoy. Dewey's mother assumed that he'd slept over at Clara's, as he did once in a while, to escape being sandwiched between his older and younger sisters. In fact, he was really staking out Seraphina's.

After a full twenty-four hours observing Seraphina and her mom undercover, Dewey felt fairly certain he had a plan to help her and was ready for a team huddle with his friends. But first he had his own mother to tackle—or rather, play a bit of defense with.

Dewey's mom sat across from him wearing her bathrobe, drinking a glass of iced coffee. She loved iced coffee, but it made her cold, so she always wore a thick, ivory bathrobe, thick socks, and her slippers in the mornings, no matter how warm it was outside.

"We stayed up late watching old movies," said Dewey. It wasn't a total lie. He had stayed up watching old movies with Clara before, just not last night. He hadn't specified *when* they'd done so when he answered his mom.

Dewey ate his cereal as he spoke to his mom. She seemed distracted by a text that had just come in on her phone. His sisters were out walking the neighbor's dog. His older sister, Stephanie, had taken it on as a job while the neighbors went out of town. His little sister, Emma, wanted to go along just because that's the sort of thing little sisters do.

"That's ridiculous. I knew she shouldn't have taken Emma with her."

"What?" asked Dewey after swallowing a bite of his cereal. Dewey had three different kinds of cereals mixed together. His mom allowed him to mix in one that had a little sugary stuff on it with the two healthier kinds. She usually did the mixing for him, but lately she'd been leaving it to him and the ratio of the sweet to the healthy had been growing in a direction he preferred.

"Pooh Bear sat down on the curb and won't walk anymore. They're out near Sycamore. Go get her, will you?" For some reason that Dewey couldn't recall anymore, they all called his little sister, Emma, Pooh Bear.

"Aw, Mom. Come on. I'm not even dressed."

"But, Dewey, the sun is in the perfect breakfast table spot! I can't go now," she implored him, settling her chin on her folded arms on the table. Like a cat, she loved a sunny spot, and it was a warm, sunny day.

Dewey sighed. "Fine. I'll go. Can I go over to Colin's after?"

"Sure," she said.

"Hey, Dews?" his mom said after a few moments.

"Yeah?"

"Want to walk over together and get her?" she conceded.

"OK."

"Alright. Just let me bundle up."

"Do you like narwhals?" Colin asked as he opened the front door for Seraphina, his voice indicating it was the secret password for entrance.

"Sure," she said. "Who doesn't like a narwhal?"

The two of them chimed in singing as she plopped her bag on the floor and herself on the couch:

"Narwhals, Narwhals,

Swimming in the ocean,

Causing a commotion,

'Coz they are so awesome . . .'

Dewey didn't think Seraphina even knew what a narwhal looked like, but the thing had caught on among them because Colin was so rhapsodic about them.

Colin's dad worked for a special effects department and each room in their apartment had two different color tones. The living room where they sat around a wooden coffee table was robin's egg blue and gold. It wasn't a big room, but it had a fireplace and a comfy couch. They liked to hang out there because Colin's dad always had good snacks and never seemed to care how much time they spent doing electronics or whatever.

Today they had a bigger problem on their hands than how to destroy zombies or build portals. They were there to save Seraphina, and Dewey thought he just might know how. So, before they looped into verse two, Dewey leapt in. "OK. I think I've got this figured out. Hand me the bowl, would ya?" he asked, pointing to some green grapes that Colin's dad had set out a few minutes before.

"Mission Octopushy," Dewey went on, popping a grape into his mouth. "You're going to have to be brave. One whole week. Tough it out. She's *got* to be tired." He popped in another grape and chewed a bit. "But," he paused, either for effect or to swallow, "she's good at what she does. I saw her. She has it down to a science, and then some. We have to get at her tired place and push her over the edge.

"So here's what you do. You are going to become *the* clingiest, hovering kid in the school—in the city—no, in the state—country, even!! Don't let up. Don't let go! She's got eight arms like an octopus, your mom! Make sure she's holding you all the time in at least one of them. Never stop. It's going to be—"

"Embarrassing!" interjected Seraphina, and Colin laughed.

"Yes," said Dewey, "but by the time we're done with her, she'll be pulling up to the curb and pushing you out the car door with one of those tentacles of hers.

"Also, you gotta start having one of those growth spurts that makes you really hungry and keeps you asking for food! Now, don't be pushy. Don't be rude! We want to string her along, nice and easy. We don't want her to give up and get mad, see? We need her to run out of steam, not blow her lid."

Colin and Seraphina looked at Dewey like he

was some sort of mad professor. When had he acquired these skills? But they had to agree—it just might work. And though Seraphina was not looking forward to all the other kids seeing her cling to her mother like a baby monkey when a lion roars, she had to admit that it couldn't be much worse than the current state of affairs.

Desperate mothers called for desperate measures.

Seraphina was in.

"Oh, Dr. Hector, I just don't know *what* to do! She won't leave me alone. Everywhere I go, she's all over me, and I mean *all* over me. She hugs my leg in the supermarket. She needs twenty hugs before bed. One hundred kisses on each cheek and fifty on her forehead. Then I have to go 'tuck, tuck, tuck' with the blanket another twenty-five. She wants to hold BOTH hands when we cross the street now. Sometimes when I drop her off somewhere, after we cross the street, she insists on crossing back with me to the car! Then I have to cross her back again. Both hands held of course. She *must* be sick," Seraphina's mom cradled the phone in the crook of her neck as she spoke to the doctor and feverishly washed and dried dishes.

"No. No fever. No. No changes. Though, wait, her appetite has increased dramatically. All I do is make her food, do her dishes, and make her food again.

"Tape worm? What's that? No, eww. Would that explain all of the hand holding?"

Seraphina's mom dried her hands on the dish towel and dragged Seraphina, who clung to her mother's leg, across the kitchen as she hung the towel up to dry on the oven door. She looked down and sighed. "OK. I'll bring her in tomorrow and have you take a look at her."

Seraphina emailed Dewey that next evening.

Hi! Update: she took me to the doctor and I passed "as healthy as a Honeycrisp apple," he said! Then I turned the cling on as soon as we left—I asked for a piggie back ride back to the car! And I had her tie my shoes this morning, but first I made sure there was a really big knot in one of them, LOL! I think I've really got the hang of this. She's just GOTTA crack soon!

Dewey replied:

Good work! Let me know if/ when it's mission accomplished. I gotta go do math. See ya!

The next morning when the kids arrived at school, Seraphina Johnson was walking herself across the street, wearing a smile as wide as the back of her mother's minivan that pulled away as she waved goodbye for the day.

"What happened?!" Colin and Dewey exclaimed.

"Mission Octopushy! You should have seen her. It was nothing like I imagined, though. I figured she might crack. Explode. Scream, yell, lose it or at least, cry. But it wasn't like that at all, in the end.

"Last night, after she tucked me in, I got up and got into her bubble bath with her—"

"You got into the bath with her?" laughed Colin.

"Yeah, listen. She had just settled into her tub, and I pulled off my PJs and plopped in. The tub was so warm and comfy and full of soft, foamy bubbles. I just slid down into it and said to her, all lovey and sweet, 'Hiya, Mom.'

"First, she stared at me like I was an alien, which, you know, could have actually made me mad if I felt like it. I'm her own daughter after all! But, whatever, I didn't get side-tracked from the mission! I said, 'I just came for some special mom and me time.'

"Then she started screaming for my dad like an intruder or a rat had just jumped into her tub. 'Ira! IIIRRRAAAA!!' My dad came rushing in, totally sure he's going to have to kill someone or something, with a baseball bat in his hand. He's all crazy and swinging it in the air at no one!

"'Get her out! Get her OUT!' my mom's screaming. And it took my dad a minute to figure out she was talking about me! He was so mad that she scared him to death, that he called 911 to pay her back!"

"Called 911?!" exclaimed Dewey.

"What happened?" cried Colin, laughing so hard that tears were starting to stream down his face. "Were you in the tub and 911 came?"

"No, because my dad was all stupid about it. He actually said what was going on to embarrass her!"

"What?" said Dewey, "'911? My wife has our daughter in the bathtub with her'?"

"Yes! That was pretty much the size of it! Then he got back in bed," narrated Seraphina.

"My mom and I jump out of the tub. She calls the police. Too late. A firetruck and an ambulance showed up at our door anyway. My dad is asleep. I'm back in my room with the covers over my head. I have no idea what she told them.

"So this morning, I didn't follow her around when she made my lunch, because I was afraid I'd maybe gone too far. But when we got to school, she just pulled up, unlocked the door, and said, 'OK, Seraphina, have a great day,' and waited for me to get out. Her eyes looked different. Tired. Sad. Done. But kind of, you know, relieved. And I had stopped hugging her leg, which I'd been doing for the last fifty-six hours, but I gave her a hug goodbye. She smiled and that was that."

And that was that.

Word spread. Dewey Fairchild was a parent problem-solver, if ever you needed one. And pretty much every kid needed one, so Dewey Fairchild became very busy. One year later he had an office, an assistant, and letterhead stationery.

Dewey Fairchild, PPS

"Mr. Fairchild, where do you think this picture should go?"

Clara Cottonwood became more than Dewey's front office assistant; she was also his hair stylist. The latter responsibility consisted of reminding her boss to comb his hair now and again, and trimming his bangs "just a titch," as she liked to say, when he started to look more mop than man.

Theirs was a symbiotic relationship—she, like those little birds on the backs of the hippos, just along for the free lunch, and he, the benefactor of her meticulous ways. Of course, Dewey Fairchild offered no real food. In fact, it was Clara Cottonwood who was baking those cookies that filled the office with the sweet smell of sugar and butter, like a mother's warm morning hug. But company was Clara's sustenance, and she enjoyed Dewey's company on those secret days they worked together. He, in turn, had a real assistant and one with many (many, many) years of experience.

"I think it looks good right over the computer on that wall. What do you think, Wolfie?"

Wolfgang von Fluff Bucket, the largest black and white Havanese this side of Cuba, cocked his head and stuck out his pink tongue more to charm than to pant. Dewey and Clara took it as an affirmative, and she nailed it in.

The fur around Wolfie's mouth was white as milk and feathery like the seed head of a dandelion. His nose looked like a big, black button sewn on a teddy bear. The rest of the fur around his eyes, head, and ears was solid black, except for his big, bushy, white eyebrows that stood out like an old man's. From his head down to his toes, a black and white fur pattern alternated so evenly that some careful child might have designed it in her coloring book: white, black, white, black.

Dewey had no idea why Clara had named him "Wolfie." He appeared a good deal more like a panda cub than a wolf—an eighteen pound fluff-ball with a cotton-candy-pink tongue.

"I've been thinking about hanging this picture for—oh, tartar sauce!" Clara had somehow managed to slam the hammer into her fore-head as she pulled it back to hit the nail, and she tumbled off the step stool onto the floor. Sadly, her "cursing" sent Dewey into a fit of laugh-ter, and, rather than helping her, he accidently tumbled over as well.

Clara stood about four foot nine, which didn't make her much taller than Dewey, and always had a smooth grey bun wrapped on top of her head. Even when she fell, her hair stayed in place. She pulled herself back up, put her small hands on her hips, and offered Dewey a hand.

"Here," she huffed, rolling her shoulders back like a soldier. "You hang it up, Papa Smurf."

Dewey hung the picture. "All done, Clara. Sorry. Really." Then, he added, "Er, sir. Ma'am," and he felt his cheeks get warm as he saluted her.

"As you were, soldier." She patted him on the shoulder warmly, and he knew they were good again, and he could go back to being the "real" boss.

It was 1600 hours when he heard the telltale sign of a client. *Pad, pad, pad. Thump! Chomp, chomp, chomp. Gulp. Pad, pad, pad . . . Thump!*

The air ducts had been set up so clients could enter unnoticed from the outside and crawl into the attic. Luckily, the house was built in the 1940s when rigid metal duct work was the norm. It was solid, just wide enough for the kids to crawl through, and there was no fiber in the air stream, which was a good thing if they wanted to breathe.

On her way in on work days, Clara placed cookies and milk at strategic locations. They served both as a welcome gesture, and also to distract any clients who might be unable to appreciate the architectural genius of rigid metal duct work used for conveyance purposes due to their claustrophobia.

She'd also fashioned herself a vent so that she could continue to bake the cookies in the attic during the day. The idea of having the oven delivered had stressed Dewey out. He just couldn't conceive of how they were going to get a 200-pound oven up the stairs of the attic without his parents knowing.

Then, one day, it was just there. When he tried to ask Clara about how she'd done it, she stuck a cookie in his mouth and smiled.

The end of the road for the client was a slide

that careened the cookie consumer directly into the office space onto a thick, soft cushion. Dewey and Clara had fashioned the slide out of wood, not plastic, as it created a more sophisticated and less "playground" feel, they'd decided. It was smooth—no splinters—and just steep enough to serve the purpose.

That construction had required Dewey and Clara to do math—rise over run—to solve the slope needed. He'd asked his dad, who prided himself on being great at math, to help him; Dewey told him it was a word problem for school. They'd had a good time figuring it out, though Dewey wished he could have had Dad help him more. The last drop was a bit abrupt if the looks on the clients' faces were any indication.

Plop! The client landed right on the big, soft, lime-green cushion next to Wolfie's cushion, which was also lime-green to accentuate his black and white coloring. Clara had set the cushion up on a small wooden platform across from Dewey's desk. They'd recently added an extra cushion, so the drop wouldn't be so abrupt. That seemed to solve the problem for the moment. They'd also added extra padding along the bottom of the duct work path, as Clara had said the spirit was willing, but the knees might start to get "fussbudgety" if some extra cushioning were not applied.

Today, with little chocolate crumbs still on the bottom right of his mouth, at 1600 hours, in plopped Danny Tedphrey. A tallish kid with mahogany red hair like an Irish Setter, Danny had dark circles under his round, wheat-brown eyes.

He looked over at Wolfie, worried.

"I have allergies. I'm allergic to acacia, elm, eucalyptus, cedar, yellow dock, common mugwort, western ragweed, cottonwood, cocklebur, Kentucky bluegrass, cultivated ryegrass, perennial ryegrass, did I say eucalyptus? Yeah, well, eucalyptus, rabbit hair, chickens, cats, and *dogs*!"

Dewey and Clara shot each other a look and not just because her last name, Cottonwood, was in his litany of allergens, though it did add to the humor of the situation.

"Who, Wolfie? Don't worry. He's hypoallergenic. He's not going to harm you at all."

Dewey then adjusted his glasses on his nose, as any good professional in any good book he'd ever read would do at this particular juncture. He didn't really wear prescription glasses, but he felt that it was good to be able to adjust them at key moments with his clients. He'd had Clara purchase a pair without a prescription for him to slip on or off and adjust when the moment seemed right.

"So, then, Danny, what brings you here today?"

Clara, who had just finished baking a batch of snickerdoodles, picked up her cue and dropped off a clipboard, pen, and this questionnaire for Danny to fill out:

Name:

Grade:

School:

Home Address:

Best Entry to Your Home Without Being Noticed:

Top Three Hiding Places in Your Home:

Siblings (names and ages):

Pets:

Parents' Names:

Problem Parent(s) Cause You:

Danny had one siblings and a pet goldfish named Sophie. He hesitated for a while trying to figure out good entry and hiding spots, but he had no problem filling out the line about problems parents cause. His father was the problem: he was a big joker. His antics weren't funny. And Danny was usually the butt of them.

"Last week while I was studying for a spelling test, he put ice down my pants. This morning he apologized for eating all of my Halloween candy last night. After I started getting all upset and yelling and stuff, then he tells me he's just kidding. Yeah. Really funny. Anyway, I want you to make him stop. That's why I'm here."

"Mmm," mused Dewey, "Halloween candy. I'd have to say my favorite ones are the Skittles. Love those. Got any of those left? I got hardly any this year. Nothing wrong with a Twizzler, either. Dark chocolate. That's what I got. Those little rectangles in the brown and red paper pledging bliss, and then all you get is bitter disappointment. Literally!"

"I like Kit Kats," Danny offered, and Clara nodded in approval as Dewey seemed to be off in his own reverie.

"Dark chocolate. What kid in his right mind wants dark chocolate? What kind of adult thinks it's a good idea to stuff dark chocolate into some kid's sack? Kit Kat? You just said Kit Kat? Now, the Japanese, they know candy! You want fruit?

Did you know they've got Kit Kat Strawberry, Kit Kat Pear, Orange, and Apple? They have Kit Kat Apricot Seed, Peach, Kiwi, Lemon, Cherry Blossom . . . Hmm, what else? Oh yeah, mix it up! Fruit Parfait. Kit Kat Pumpkin, hello! Halloween, people! Kit Kat Watermelon and Salt. Now, you gotta admit that's inspired, sweet and salty."

Before Danny could interject anything—not that he could think of a thing to say—Clara rolled up a chair for him to sit down in and tried, unsuccessfully, to make eye contact with Dewey, who had begun another pace around the desk and continued, "No good, you say? You're more in a veggie mood? Sweet Potato, Edamame, and even Hot Chili Pepper! They have Kit Kats that rival Clara's cookies, even—sorry, Clara! Kit Kat Cinnamon Cookies! Or a Strawberry or Blueberry Cheesecake Kit Kat!"

Clara put a finger up to try and get a word in—her mouth opened, but before she could speak Dewey said, "Say, all this talk of eating Kit Kats is making me thirsty." Dewey sat down in his chair, next to Clara and across from Danny. "I think I'll have a Green Tea Kit Kat! Or some milk—"

An elderly elbow landed squarely in Dewey's left rib and he stopped short.

"Right. Practical jokes. No good. Must stop him. Got it. On the case. You've come to the right place, Danbear. Let's get started."

Clara placed a fresh cookie and a glass of milk down. Part of the operation was to parcel out different flavors and textures of cookies one at a time. It kept the clients engaged while not allowing them to get too full too fast, though Clara wondered if Dewey's Kit Kat tangent hadn't just made all of this just seem a bit too simple.

"Oh," Clara inquired. "I suppose I should have asked this earlier. Food allergies?"

"Nope," Danny replied as he bit into a chewy oatmeal cookie filled with M&Ms. Wolfie got his without M&Ms and wagged his tail, which was curled up behind and over his back like a wire hanger covered with snowy tinsel.

"I need a list of your dad's favorite things—his favorite foods, hobbies, whatever. Anything that you can think of that he gets excited about, I want to know it. We'll have him taken care of in no time."

"OK," said Danny. "Is that it?"

"Yes, for now," said Dewey. "We'll talk more after I get this profile information."

"OK, um, well, thanks for the cookies and the help. I'll get back to you about my dad's favorite stuff."

Danny went out the way he came in. Sort of. Admittedly, this was the least smooth part of their operation.

Clara hurried over and placed a thick wooden board lined with shelf paper ("to class it up a bit") atop the cushion right under the chute. She threaded her fingers together and provided

Danny a step and hoist up to climb back in the way he came.

Why they didn't just provide a step stool or build a ladder is anyone's guess. But the first time Dewey suggested it, Clara balked saying, "I'm as strong as an eastern lowland gorilla. I don't see wasting materials when we're all set."

And it was kind of endearing each time she put her hands together like a ranch hand helping a kid mount a horse.

When Danny's feet pulled up and away, Dewey leaned back in his chair and put his feet up on the desk.

"OH! I totally forgot Kit Kat Tiramisu!" he said to Clara. "Dark chocolate. Hmph."

"I don't know, sir. I think I'd prefer dark chocolate over a potato bar—ha!! Get it, potato bar? Now that's kind of funny!" she laughed and left to take care of some things at home.

As Dewey sat at his desk, he wondered if the Japanese cut the crust off of their sandwiches. He bet they did.

Well, enough of that—he had to start figuring out how to fix up Danny's dad.

He leaned over and gave Wolfie a belly rub for inspiration, and Wolfie made some noise that sounded a lot like "Rarara" which made Dewey feel all soft and warm inside. He sighed and stared deeply at the picture he and Clara had just hung on the wall and began to think.

The Plan

"What ore you doween?" Dewey's little sister Emma had spotted him on his iPad. Now he'd never get anything done.

His four-year-old sister had large, almond-shaped eyes. One evening they had played a family game of picking what color everyone's eyes were in the big box of Crayola crayons and Emma's, they decided, looked "Denim." Emma, aka, Pooh Bear, had milky white skin, this little kitten nose, and, messy, soft, long brown hair, and, if anyone had bothered to pick a crayon color for her lips, they'd be "Pig Pink." She was downright adorable. She was also downright annoying.

Perhaps even more unfortunate, though, was the fact that Pooh Bear was stronger than he was, which, as you can imagine, humiliated him occasionally. OK, maybe a lot of the time. She had some letter problems which made her sound like a baby, but that didn't seem to make her any less tough.

One time, a runny-nosed brat tried to steal Dewey's Transformer, and she put a swift elbow to that kid's ear, grabbed it back, and then went right back in for his GoGurt. She was just two. Emma didn't mess around.

"Nothing. Just some stuff."

"What kind of stuff? Can I pway?"

"I'm not playing. I'm working. Can you bug off?"

"Yes! I wuh be a wady bug!! 'Wady Bug Wady Bug fwwwy away . . .' Hey, Dewey?"

"Yeah?"

"What ore you doween?"

"Some research." He sighed. "Do you want to help?"

"Yes! Oh yes! I want to hewp, Dewey. Hey, Dewey? Can I hewp?"

"I just said you can help! Here. Hold this. Now press this button. See? The cars are loading. We want to see if we can find the nicest red Corvette for sale online."

"I wike wed wowipops."

"Ha! I'll bet you do! I wonder if I can find one right about now."

Dewey went to his Halloween stash and managed to find a green one.

"Will green do?"

Two nods of the head later and that kid was licking and sucking like a pool filter when the water level is low.

"You said your dad is into cars, especially Corvettes. Be sure you load his iPad to this page so next time he opens it, that's what pops up," explained Dewey. He was talking softly under the orange tree in Danny's back yard. The air felt hot today, and the shade brought a welcome break from the heat.

"And that's it? Then what?"

"Then just wait. It's better if you don't know too much. It's easier for you to not let on you know something when you don't, well, know something . . ." That sounded funny to Dewey's ear when he heard himself say it, so he added, "If you know what I mean," and pushed his mock glasses up on his nose.

"Just do what I've said and let me know what happens," continued Dewey. "Place the iPad and watch what he does. If he takes the bait the way I think he will, we'll be set. Report what happens to me. Don't call. Don't email. Wolfie will be waiting here under this tree with a small recorder around his neck. Come out and pet him, hit record, and whisper to him all that you know. Oh, and feed him a snack for his troubles, would ya? Sliced carrots are good. Then send him on his way and just wait."

"Got it: iPad, observe, carrots, pet dog, whisper. Roger that!"

"Say, speaking of snacks, you have anything? I'm starving."

Royal Peas and Carrots

"He did it, Wolfie! Oh, help! Is this thing on? How do I know if this thing is on?!" Danny whispered, with a panicked voice, into Wolfie's fur as he fed him an entire carrot under the orange tree. He fumbled around to try, with his less capable left hand, to turn on the recorder.

"A-hem," he began again, trying to regain his composure and tapping on the recorder. "He did it. My dad opened his iPad and saw the Corvette. He—" *Crunch, crunch, crunch.* The sound of Wolfie eating carrots was all that Clara could hear. She reviewed the recording again.

"A-hem. He did it. Dad opened his iPad and saw the Corvette. He—" *Crunch, crunch, crunch.*

"Wolfie!" she exclaimed. Wolfie lifted his head from the chair where he was resting and looked, anticipating something of interest.

Clara imagined exactly what that moment with Danny must have looked like: Wolfie, with his pink little tongue and the wag of his feathery tail, crunching and munching on the carrot like a hippity happy bunny rabbit.

She sighed and started the recorder again. More heavy breathing and whispering.

"So I don't know why that would matter, but then he surfed and clicked around a bit more and a lot of—" *Crunncchhh, mmmccchh.*

"Aw, fruit flies and bananas! What'd you go and tell that boy to give him carrots for? I can't make out a thing he's saying, sir!"

"That's OK, Clara," replied Dewey, unconcerned. "Just take notes on what you've got, and let me know when you're done. Wolfie was really mostly there just to keep Danny calm. We'll get all the information we need when we see him later." At the mention of his name again, Wolfie pranced over and out came that pink tongue again. Dewey swore that dog was smiling. His pink tongue, if Dewey matched it to the Crayola box, would be "Tickle Me Pink"; it curved softly like the small bowl of a wet spoon, thickly outlined in black.

"Yeah, yeah. You're a good boy." Dewey snuggled his face into the soft fur, and in return got a pink lick right on his nose. Wolfie, who had returned to his sleeping moments before, had his fur flattened on his face.

"Hold still," said Dewey as he snapped a picture of him. He texted it to Colin with the message #derpy, followed by a message telling him he was ready to work on their social studies project now.

They had to build an historic mission without

using sugar cubes, mud, flour, clay, glue, or a writing utensil or computer. *How do teachers dream up this nonsense?* Dewey wondered as they sat there, banging their heads against the wall with no good ideas. Literally. Colin had arrived an hour and a half before and was now hitting his head against the wall, while Dewey laughed.

"Maybe if you get enough lumps on your head we can use that as the foundation."

"I gotta go home and rest. I need some cookies. Can I have some cookies?" asked Colin.

Dewey sighed, lifting a cover off of a plate of fresh, warm cookies. "Go home. Be a quitter. But don't blame me when you're building your mission out of canned peas and honey."

Colin filled both fists with cookies and stuffed one in his mouth for good measure.

"—uy ara! Ee you ater," he managed to articulate before he went down the attic stairs to use the front door, like a regular house guest. "Canned peas and honey. That's not half bad," Dewey heard him saying as he left.

Oh brother, thought Dewey and he turned his attention now to Clara. "So, Clara. Whadya manage to decipher?"

"Mr. Fairchild, as far as I can decipher between crunches," she shot a glare Wolfie's way, "Danny's father has, indeed, clicked our link."

"Great!" exclaimed Dewey. "Then let's get that letter sent out to him and begin phase two."

"Already have it cued, sir," she went on. "Oh. And, if I'm not overstepping here, how about a mission built out of mini-marshmallows and caramel sauce and some royal icing? Maybe some big marshmallows here and there? I think that might do a lot more nicely than Mr. Colin's head."

"What's royal icing?" asked Dewey. "It sounds regal."

"It's what I use to decorate the holiday cookies. It gets hard as cement! It holds ginger-bread houses together, that's what made me think of it! I've taken the liberty to get you a simple recipe for it," she added, handing him a sheet with the step by step instructions.

"Clara, you're a genius!" cried Dewey as he threw his arms around her.

"Oh, it's nothing, Mr. Fairchild," but her little old lady cheeks turned red as apples in the fall.

Mission Accomplished

When the letter arrived, Danny was downstairs at the kitchen table trying to sew together burlap pieces to somehow make them into a stuffed Cuddle-Pet mission. He wasn't very good with a needle and thread, and he'd already poked his finger about three times. His fingers were covered in Band-Aids, which wasn't adding to his dexterity. The dark circles under his eyes really made him look beaten up.

He'd taken in Wolfie, undercover, to "pet sit," and he knew his next steps: wait for the letter to arrive, turn on the recorder, and play dumb.

That wasn't too hard since he didn't know much about what was going on. Anyway, he felt more stressed about how to make the four walls of his stuffed mission hold up than he was about his dad at this moment.

"ARRRGGHHH!"

As Danny pulled the needle through the burlap, his father's scream across the house stabbed into his own silence and concentration so jarringly that he physically jumped in his chair, felt his heart race, and his fingertips tingle, all in a matter of seconds. Even Wolfie started and let out a spontaneous bark, the one that he reserved for strangers at the door and possible danger. His father's yell sounded like he must have severed an entire ear shaving!

When Danny ran to see what had happened, he found his father with the letter in his hand and he knew.

Then he panicked.

He hid himself in the bathroom, trembling with fear. Soon though, he heard scratching at the door. *Scratch.* Danny ignored it, still too scared to come out. *Scratch, scratch.* Then the scratching got more frantic, and then came whining. Danny was forced to open the door.

"OK, Wolfie, OK!" Danny's face looked almost as red as his hair as he let Wolfie in with him, but the dog refused, insisting Danny instead come out. When he finally did, he found his father with his head down on the kitchen table. He wasn't sure, but Danny was pretty sure that his father was about to—no, wait, yes! His father was crying!

"Argh!" He blubbered. "What the Top Ramen have I done?! A $500,000 Corvette?! I purchased it? But all I did was click 'get more information.' No! No! No!"

He wailed and pounded his fist on the table rhythmically, a man beating his own tragic drum song.

"What am I going to tell your mother?!" Snot ran down his nose, mixed with his tears, and made a soupy, soppy, slobbery mess. Danny quickly gathered up his social studies project out of the way of his father's flying fist and freely flowing snot and tears. Ugh, too late. An edge of the bell tower got snot dripped right on it. Maybe it'll look like bird poop, thought Danny, trying to make the best out of a clearly out-of-control situation.

Somehow, in all of this, Danny began to not feel quite *so* bad. It seemed Wolfie didn't know that, though. He rubbed up against Danny's leg, insisting Danny pet him. Danny, more interested in his father's scene, ignored Wolfie, which prompted that black and while ball of fluff to escalate his strategy.

First the leg rub. Strike. Then the charm. He placed his head on Danny's knee. Strike two. Totally insulted when cuteness failed, he growled and that got Danny's attention. Danny threw him a bone, so to speak, and gave him a stroke or two.

"I'm fine, boy," he said quietly.

That seemed to settle Wolfie down momentarily. Then another growl. Pet again. Growl again. Pet again. Danny noticed Wolfie's fur was as soft as one of his big sister's favorite coats; she always got mad when he touched it, saying he'd get it dirty. Wolfie felt more like a cat than a dog when he petted him. His mind went back to his hysterical father, and his hand moved up to run through his own hair mindlessly. Wolfie started to make a low guttural sound in his throat again.

"Geez, sorry!" said Danny. As he nervously stroked Wolfie again, his fingers rubbed up against a little piece of paper in the fluffy fur. Wolfie released an audible exhale through his nose and lay down. His work was finally done. Someone needed to throw him a real bone. But Danny was way too nervous to notice any needs Wolfie might have. Wolfie could tell he wasn't getting a treat any time soon, so he just closed his eyes to rest. Danny unfolded the note and read it:

Turn on Wolfie's camera now. Wait 5 minutes, and then tell your dad it's a prank.

Wolfie stood back up. Five more minutes then. That was a short-lived nap.

Danny took a deep breath and obeyed. Then he sat back and watched his dad blubber like a big baby. He'd never seen so many different forms of crying.

First he stood there reading the letter muttering quietly over and over, "$500,000, $500,000."

Then he got up on top of the kitchen table and grabbed whatever was close by and yelled, "No," as he threw a fork. "No!" There went a spoon. "No!" Another fork. When he ran out of silverware to throw, he threw himself down and curled up in a ball on the floor and sucked his thumb!

"Dad," Danny cried. "Dad?!" He was beginning to feel a bit awful and more than a bit worried. Thankfully, for the good of the plan, his dad seemed unable to hear anything Danny said, and just lay there, in his little ball on the floor, sucking his thumb.

And then five minutes were up.

So Danny said it. He took a deep breath, met his dad's puffy red eyes straight on, and said, "Dad. Just kidding. Gotcha!" Danny forced a too big, widemouthed smile as he shuffled his feet just a bit and did a little ta-da move. His feet showed a lot more confidence than his voice.

The tape stopped there. Danny ran upstairs to escape his dad and any reaction he might have to face. Wolfie sprinted home, too.

The video went viral. Dewey posted it on YouTube, and it got over 10,000 hits within the first twenty-four hours and 1,000 subscribers.

Within forty-eight hours, Danny and his dad

were on the news.

"When we return: one father's near encounter with utter ruin, only it was all a big joke. Can children abuse their parents? When we get back . . ."

"Well, Mr. Tedphrey, there were a lot of responses to that video. Some parents found it hilarious. Others felt that your son humiliated you and showed you great disrespect, crossed a line into parental abuse, even. Do you think that children today think that pranking is more acceptable given the widespread audience that YouTube and the like provides?" The lights were shining brightly into Danny's eyes as Marcia Mauley interviewed the father and son.

"Well, Marcia, I'm afraid, as they say, 'the stink bomb doesn't fall very far from the stinker.'"

"Ah ha, ha, ha! Sorry. You'll have to explain that to our audience or, at least, to this newscaster."

"Let's put it another way, then," explained

Danny's dad. "The rotten egg doesn't squeeze out very far from the rotten chicken's egg chute."

Danny wiggled and squirmed in his seat. The lights were hot, and his dad was definitely starting to embarrass him on national television. *Geez!* was the totality of Danny's thoughts at that moment.

"Am I to understand that you're—ahem—the rotten chicken's egg chute in this analogy then, Mr. Tedphrey?"

"I'm afraid so. The point is, Marcia, I've been playing pranks on this kid since before he could walk or talk. I used to play them on my friends and brother. And then, when I became a dad, well, it's just such fun when you're the guy doing the prank. You know what I mean? Turns out though, it's not such fun to be the guy on the receiving end. No, I can't be mad about this. I brought it on myself," Danny's dad continued. "Listen, I'm just so relieved I don't actually own a $500K Corvette."

"And the utter and complete humiliation and embarrassment of you crying like a baby? Throwing things? *Sucking your thumb?*" continued Marcia Mauley in dismay.

"Yeah. That part sucks. Ha! Get it? Sucks! Sorry. I won't deny it. But what you gonna do? As I said, stink bomb, stinker. I'll tell you this much, though. My pranking days are done. If you can't take it, don't dish it out. I can't take it."

"Danny," Marcia turned to him along with four camera guys and their lenses. "Any last words from you?"

Danny felt a red hot glow spread up his ears and face.

"I'm allergic to chickens."

Michael

Dewey's older sister, Stephanie, had all the real brains in the family, and she must have been OK looking. Dewey noticed boys were always hanging around her. His sister was too busy studying and getting As to even care about them, or him.

She had won the PEAP (that's the Presidential Educational Awards Program) last year. He wasn't sure what she'd go for after that. There was probably someone important to impress after the president though, like the Prime Minister of the Universe or something, and she'd go for that.

Stephanie was sitting on Dewey, trying to help him with his math homework. That's right, she was sitting on him. Because he hated math problems when they were long. And he hated when his mother had her help him even more.

Phanie, as he'd taken to calling her these days, had him face down in the carpet and she sat on his butt. She was riding him like one of those big tortoises, but he didn't have a thick shell. Plus, the fuzz from the carpet was getting squashed into and tickling his nostrils and burning his cheek.

Dewey's dad knocked on the door.

"Everything OK in there?" he called as he opened the door and saw Stephanie, her hair pulled back in a smooth brown ponytail, sitting atop Dewey.

"Yeah, just helping Dewey with his math," she said, as if sitting on his bottom and squishing his face was the general way people helped with homework.

"Oh! I want to help, Dewey! Can I help?" asked Dewey's dad as he knelt.

"I don't need anybody's help!" protested Dewey.

"Suit yourself, genius," and she was off like a swimsuit cover up on a sunny day at the beach.

"Darn it," Dewey grumbled into the carpet. All signs now pointed to him doing his math with his dad for at least an hour. His dad *loved* to do homework with him, and seemed to make math take twice as long just to relish the experience together.

Dewey stood up and put the paper on his desk. "That's OK, Dad. I got it. I'll let you know if I need help later. I've got some other stuff I want to do."

"You sure? I have time now." His dad was already settling in at Dewey's desk. "You never let me do math with you anymore. Come on! It'll be fun. Or I can do it for you! Don't tell Mom. It'll be our secret."

"Maybe later, Dad. OK?"

"Oh, sure, the Cheshire cat smile," Dewey's dad smiled back as he got up from the desk. "I can take a hint." He patted Dewey on the head and left him to his own devices.

When Dewey made his way into the attic, he found Clara under a pile of papers searching for something and looking a bit harried.

"Clara?"

"Oh, Boss! Thank goodness. We've got a total backlog of cases here, and I can't put my finger on the one that came in last night when you went home for dinner."

Clara rummaged around the pile of papers some more, blowing hard at a piece of wispy grey hair that kept landing in her eyes as they darted and scanned the desk like they were chasing a fly. Wolfie cocked his head sideways, watching her.

"That's all very nice, Wolfie, dear, but why the kitty whiskers don't you *do* something to help me?"

Wolfie gave a sneeze. *Ahptttoooo*! Then another. *Ahptttoooo*. He sneezed to get someone to throw his favorite pet skunk toy or to pet him. Dewey grabbed his skunk, which looked like a miniature version of Wolfie himself, and threw it across the room. Wolfie ran off to go fetch it, but rather than bringing it back, he settled down in his cushioned bed with it and a sigh.

Clara let out a sigh of her own, though hers was really more of a huff.

"It was a memo from Michael de la Cruz . . . said something about needing your expertise, immedia—Merlin's pants! *Where* is it?!" she exploded as she dumped the recycle basket over and began going through it page by page.

"Are you sure it came in as a faxed memo? Michael likes to text," offered Dewey.

"TEXT! Yes, text! That's it. Cheese Whiz! Just *look* at this place. I'm sorry, Mr. Fairchild. I'll have it cleaned up in no time. Now, where is that phone?" she muttered, digging under her piles and piles of papers.

Dewey shot a smiling glance toward Wolfie who would have rolled his eyes if he could have, but instead wiggled his behind deeper into the cushion and rested his chin on the edge.

"Got it, sir."

It read more like Morse code than a text.

To Whom It May Concern Colon

[stop]

My mother is going to kill me with hygiene.

[stop]

I'm sure the irony is not missed.

[stop]

I have herd you have a way with people's mothers and the ways they are their children's undoing

Herd not herd

Herd not herd!!

HEARD

[stop]

[end]

Please advise

Sent from my mobile phone while speaking and walking into stuff. Typos a given.

Dewey remembered Michael de la Cruz from Franklin last year. He was your basic middle school girl's prince charming. Handsome, astute, skin as clear as Silly Putty when you first open the egg.

Dewey had those little red eggs of Silly Putty squirreled away all over his house and office. Silly Putty didn't have that great smell that made you almost want to eat it like Play-Doh, but he got incredible satisfaction rolling it in a perfect ball in his hands. He liked to roll it and roll it until it was one hundred percent smooth and round, like a large marble.

Dewey realized some people enjoyed the stretch of it—a quick pull of Silly Putty and it snapped—a long, slow pull and it would string like gum. But Dewey always found that strategy messy and not nearly as satisfying. He did have to agree with one aspect of the Silly Putty stretch camp . . . the intense satisfaction that one got squeezing it back together after stringing it out and those little air bubbles like a miniature cap-gun going off. They made the tiniest little snap, the kind his mother and aunt made while they sat chatting and chewing their gum.

Dewey would bet that Michael de la Cruz didn't have Silly Putty around his house. But, handsome, talented, older, and clear-skinned as he was, he had a problem and was coming to Dewey for help. This was a big day, indeed. Even his sister would have to be impressed.

When Michael slid into the office, Wolfie seemed to know he was in the presence of a godlike creature, and he rolled over and offered his belly for a rub.

"I'll be a monkey's uncle," said Clara. "He

never does that for strangers." She offered Michael some cookies, but he declined, saying he'd had more than his delicious fill on his way through the air ducts.

AHPTTOO. AHPTTOO. Wolfie, on the other hand, gave two short quick sneezes, and looked expectantly.

"Cute dog," smiled Michael warmly.

"Here," offered Clara, "give him this. He'll be yours for life." Michael popped an oatmeal cookie in Wolfie's mouth.

Wolfie took the cookie, stored it in his cheek like a chipmunk, and went off to his cushion to eat it.

"Huh. Cute dog," he said again. "So, is Dewey around? I'm eager to get this started."

On cue, Dewey walked in making himself look just a little busier than he really was by finishing up a pretend phone call.

"Right. Got it. Thank you so much. Mm, bye bye."

"Oh, hey, Michael. Good to see you," he said, extending his hand and shaking Michael's. "I've got your paperwork. I like that PDF app you have on your phone. Very nice."

"Yeah, thanks. So—"

"Right. Let's get started," said Dewey as he took a seat and ushered Michael into one of his own. "So, this has been going on since you were three years old, you say?"

"Oh, well, I'm sure it's been going on always. It's just that I can't really remember too much before that. But, for as long as I can remember, my mom has been crazy about germs. During flu season she carries a bottle of bleach with her to the grocery store and won't take the cookies or cereal off the shelf without spraying them down first. She won't let me push a traffic light or elevator button without using sanitizer on my hands afterwards. When I go to the doctor's office, we have to wait in the car before she sneaks me into a room . . . even when I'm the one sick! It never ends.

"What does *your* mom do when you throw up, Dewey?" continued Michael.

"I guess she holds my forehead and my hair out of the way if I make it to the toilet. Otherwise, she grabs a bowl, and same drill."

"My mom waits for me to finish, pushes me out of the bathroom with one hand and sprays the Lysol with the other."

"Oh. I see. Is she generally a person lacking in compassion and so unkind?" Dewey inquired. He was starting to take some notes. This case was shaping up to be a bit more complicated than some of his others.

"No, that's the thing. She's really nice and loving. Until she gets all freaked out about germs. Then she's like some Dr. Jekyll and Mr. Hyde. Two nights ago, I was out on the porch with Sally Frones, and I give her an innocent kiss on her cheek good night, and Mr. Hyde comes springing out on us, like some crazy electrocuted cat with her hair all on end and a washcloth in her hands, and starts scrubbing our cheeks and lips. I seriously wanted to die.

"Sally ran home, of course. I don't even know what to tell her. I'm just going to say my mom has a mentally ill twin. Anyway. You can help, right?"

"Right," Dewey nodded with confidence even though he was feeling, for the first time in his long career, a bit of doubt.

"Let's talk tomorrow." Dewey ushered Michael back out the way he came and sat down. He stuck a cookie in his mouth and chewed slowly.

"Clara, this one is going to take some thought. Hold all my calls."

Hyde and Seek

At eleven years old, Dewey still preferred to climb in bed with his mom many nights and have her read to him before he fell asleep. He liked his parents' bed. It was so big you could always move around and find an untouched, cool spot. The sheets were softer and more crisp than his own, and there were many more pillows. It just felt inviting and good to be there.

Sometimes, when his mom was tired and willing, she'd even let him fall asleep in her bed after she read the story to him, and then his dad would carry him back to his own bed. Lots of times, though, he wasn't tired enough yet and would want to keep reading his own book after she was done, and they'd kiss him goodnight in his own bed.

That evening, when Dewey came in, his mom was propped up high on pillows reading her own book: *How to Parent Your Ten- to Fourteen-Year-Old*.

"That's funny! Are you reading about how to deal with me?" laughed Dewey.

"Oh, sure. Laugh it up, mister."

He patted her on the head. "Good Mom," he said.

She laughed, set her book down on the nightstand, and picked up the book they'd been reading together. She was under about five blankets, so Dewey snuggled under just the top one. After about a page into it, she suddenly stopped reading.

"There," she said.

"What?" asked Dewey, confused.

"That smell. There it is again. Don't you smell it? Cookies! Or cake! I'm telling you, the neighbors are always baking something over there. I think we should get to know them better! I need to get myself a cupcake. Or a donut. I need a plate of cookies right now."

"Yeah," said Dewey, trying to divert her attention because she actually sounded serious. "You haven't baked in a while. How come?"

"That's true. It's been a while." She set the book down on her chest. "Anything new at school? Any good pillow talk?"

Pillow talk is what they used to call it when Dewey was younger and would fall asleep with her sometimes. Once the lights were out he'd tell her about things that were on his mind—when the kindergarten teacher had said "shut up" which he knew was a bad word, or when he had eaten ants with Grandpa and wondered if that was OK.

Right now, though, he didn't have too much on his mind except Michael's case, and he actually kind of just wanted to hear what was going to happen next in the story.

"Would it be OK if you just read a little bit more, Mom?"

"Oh, sure, honey. Of course."

She started to read no more than a line. Then, right in the middle of her sentence, "Don?" she called out his dad's name.

She picked up reading again until Dewey's dad came in.

"Did you call me? Oh, you guys look sweet. Can I get you something?"

"Yes, as a matter of fact, I need a cookie. Or something. A slice of cake would do. Not ice cream. Something baked. Don't you smell it? Dewey, want anything?"

"I'll just suck on some ice, thanks," Dewey, having consumed his fill of cookies for the day already, felt ill at the idea of anything sweet right now.

She picked up the book and read to him until she'd had her way with a big slice of chocolate pie that his dad actually had to run to the corner store to get her. By the time she'd finished the pie and the chapter, Dewey had yawned a six breather—you know, the kind that goes in long and slowly and comes out in six parts, *Aaa-uuu-ooo-www-hhh-nnn.*

His dad put his hand on his back and led him in the direction of his room.

"Bedtime for Bonzo," he said.

"Hey!" cried Mom as Dewey walked out. "Kiss, please."

He backed up and offered her his sleepy cheek.

"Night, Sweet-pie."

"Good night, Mom."

As Dewey lay in his own bed though, he began thinking about the case and found himself less sleepy again. Dewey's mom read him books that he could have truthfully read to himself, but he probably never would. He liked when she read them to him.

They'd gotten through the first three Harry Potter books when he was younger and they'd both loved them. But the end of the third one was so scary that Dewey had to ask her to only read it during the day, and so she'd decided that they should wait until he was a bit older to continue with the rest.

Tonight they were in the middle of reading *Tom Sawyer* and, while there was a murder, graves, and even a "Potter" of its own, it was nothing by today's standards.

Dewey got to thinking about Tom. He wondered what help Tom Sawyer would have needed from Dewey. Tom seemed like he could handle his own affairs. That kid had grit, alright. Dewey loved the part in the story where he takes the blame at school for the book that Becky rips, and then she loves him.

He wondered if he'd really be willing to get paddled at school just for a girl. He probably would be too scared. He'd rather hide. Just like he was hiding from his mom that the cookies she smelled were his; just like he was hiding from his friends that he was too scared to read Harry Potter but he—hide. Hide! HYDE! Michael had said his mom was like Mr. Hyde. What was *she* hiding? Was there something she was hiding that explained why she became such a crazy germ freak of a mother?

Dewey turned on his light and took out his notebook. Michael had said it started when he was three but assumed it was because that's as far back as he could recall. But maybe something had happened. He had to find out what secret she hid.

Dewey looked at the clock. It was late. Too late to text. But, he reasoned, Michael could just answer in the morning.

Hey, Michael.

He paused to compose and was surprised to get a reply.

Hey.

Oh, you're up! Then he regretted typing out "you're" instead of "ur". He didn't have to look like a doofus to be professional.

M: Indeed

D: Here's what I need you 2 do. Go out 2 lunch with your mom. Special time. Just the 2 of you. I'll send you with a list of questions to ask her. Be prepared 2 share personal stuff. It will help.

M: Roger that.

He fired off a bitmoji of himself in bed that said "Good night."

Out, from Michael.

Now he just had to figure out what questions would get Michael's mother to open up and share. Yeah. He was going to need help. Maybe his sister could help, but she was just so annoying about any sort of assistance. Clara could help, but she seemed a bit distracted right now. He needed her focused on her post. *Seraphina? Sure, why not? Yes.* He'd ask her in the morning.

The Mastermind

"Well, it's the least I can do," Seraphina said, pouring milk over the cookie cereal that Clara was testing out. Small, nickel-sized cookies, three flavors: red velvet, oatmeal with chocolate chips, and ginger snaps, were floating in a round, clear glass bowl.

"Yummm. This is good," Seraphina said between bites. "You should sell it!"

"Nonsense, my dear. It's what we do here! I am trying to decide, though, if it's over the top to serve it with chocolate milk."

"I like it this way," replied Seraphina. "Just plain milk. Too sweet with chocolate, I think," she smiled, feeling very glad to have her opinion sought on the matter.

Seraphina only had one class with Dewey that year, and they sat at opposite sides of the U. It was Spanish class. So far, the one thing she'd learned how to say well was "*chicle en la basura*" which meant "gum in the trash."

As opposed to many of her sillier classmates who got reprimanded for goofing off (present CEO of this winning company not excluded), Seraphina was more of what you'd call a silent offender. Her outfits were always just so. Her hair was the sort that looked as if it had never been colored out of the lines. Maybe that's why it entertained her to be just a little bit less than "just so," now and again, as she would try to get away with chewing gum hidden between her upper gum line and her teeth or tucked up into her cheek like a chipmunk.

Inevitably, though, she'd get bored and forget it was there. Then, before you knew it, it was *chicle en la basura* time. She probably got caught with gum at least twice a week. Other than that one (admittedly repeat) offense, she was, indeed, a model student.

Seraphina felt pretty honored and excited to be sitting in Dewey's office, not as a client, but as a resource, eating cookie cereal and offering her opinion on this undercover assignment.

"I need to get her to talk about memories. So Michael is going to have a special lunch with her. But I need to help him get her to talk. How do you think this might work? What do you think he should say?"

"Well, why can't he just ask her about stuff. You know, 'Mom, how old was I when I first walked?' That kind of thing. Oh! I know! How about if he asks her to go through his baby book with him. I did that with my mom on my birthday once. That was fun."

"Good. Gooood!" Dewey burst out as he clicked a pen against his bottom teeth. "That's the thinking I needed. Girl stuff."

"Dewey. That's kind of sexist, you know?"

"Oh. Sorry. I didn't mean it to sound sexy," Dewey said, turning three shades of red and completely confounded. "Why would that be sexy?"

"Hahahaha! No, silly! Not sexy, sexist. You know, prejudiced against women. Why does looking at a baby book *have* to be girl stuff? I'm just saying th—"

"Oh. Right. Yeah. Of course. I mean, I guess so. OK, I meant no disrespect. How's that?"

"Sure, yeah. Whatever. I'm still here. I think that can work, if your guy Michael can handle pulling it off."

"Oh, sure," Dewey replied before pouring himself a bowl of cookie cereal. "It's not that hard, I imagine. But then how do we get her to get to the Mr. Hyde part? You know, the part that she's not talking about all these years. I doubt that's in the baby book."

"Right," Seraphina said. "So you gotta have him ask questions like, 'So I walked at ten months. Did I have any big falls?' 'Oh, so I got my first tooth when I was six months? Did I bite anyone?' That kind of thing. He should pepper those questions in along with the good, fun stuff they talk about."

"Hmm. I better send Wolfie to record this. This is good. This is better than good. This is great, actually. Seraphina, you are a genius."

Seraphina smiled at Dewey and turned three shades of red.

Michael didn't need Wolfie to record it. He said he'd use his iPhone to do it himself.

They made a plan to keep in touch via text during his special lunch with his mom in case he needed help. Dewey had Seraphina on call, also via text, and he had his phone on his desk with

Clara monitoring it for any action.

Saturday came and Michael had his lunch with his mother. He learned a lot about his many years of life thus far. He was pretty impressed with what he'd discovered. In fact, he was considering writing his autobiography after this lengthy conversation with his mother. After all, he'd walked and talked impressively early. At two months old he said, "ah-goo." He was drawing pictures at twelve months old (OK, he was eating the crayons, but so what, he could draw!).

His mother shared with him "quotables" from his baby book. At three years old he'd said, "Hey, Dad! You're sitting on one side of the table, and I'm on the other side. That's ironic!" OK, so not quite irony, but not bad for three years old. *Now there's a mastermind in the making!* Michael thought.

But the information that proved most helpful was the story she shared about the cat litter box.

"Oh, it was one of my worst days in mothering ever," she recalled. "You were probably nine months old, and I was doing the dishes. The whole house was completely childproof as far as I was concerned, so you were allowed to crawl around the living room by yourself, and I'd left you there with your toys. When I turned off the garbage disposal the house was quiet. Disturbingly quiet. So I went to look for you in the living room, but you weren't there. I went around the whole house—which, as you'll recall, was just a little one at the time, so you couldn't have gotten far—but it didn't matter, because you had found yourself some danger, nonetheless.

"Our cat litter box had a lid on it. You know the kind. It was like a little plastic house, a sandbox with a roof and an opening for the cat to crawl into. We kept it in the laundry room. Well, that's where I found you. Just your feet, actually, as the rest of you burrowed your way into the litter box like a puppy digging up a flower garden! Oh, I just shudder to even think of it now! I lifted the lid off to get you, and, to my horror, I found you with a big grin on your face munching and crunching on cat poo and litter!

"I screamed! I thought you'd cry I screamed so loudly. But you just sat there munching and crunching, little litter crumbs on your cheeks and a big proud smile on your face. I dragged you out of the box. Pulled the cat poop out of your mouth, scrubbed your tongue with a baby wipe, and made you rinse with mouthwash (*then* you began crying!). I called the emergency Poison Control Center.

"'Don't worry,' they said. 'Not the first time this has happened. He'll be fine.'

"But I was horrified," his mother's eyes teared up now, "and I just couldn't forgive myself for having let you out of my sight and for not putting a gate in front of the door."

The lunch didn't end on that tragic tale. Michael managed to ask her about his first time making her laugh hard, and she recalled the time his father dropped a heavy book on his foot and yelled out a four letter word that rhymed with duck, and Michael started quacking.

Michael joked that maybe "duck, duck, goose" wasn't such a great game for kids, after all!

They both had a good laugh over that, finished their lemonade, and Michael gave his mom a quick hug.

"Thanks, Mom!" he called out and headed off to his room to make sure the recording had come out OK.

"Don't forget to wash your hands when you go in!" she called out after him.

Michael went in, washed his hands, sent the recording to Dewey, and sat back to wait for Dewey to work his magic. He sure hoped he could.

Clara's Roll

Well, neither Michael nor Dewey had texted her, so they must not have needed her help.

Seraphina texted Colin instead and asked him if he'd heard from Dewey, but he was away for winter break and hadn't.

She decided she'd just go over to his office and see how things were going.

The crawl through the air ducts smelled sweet as always. She was glad that she had not eaten before going over, as her tummy craved a little something sweet just about then. As she made her way through the passage, a red, laminated, neatly-lettered sign blocked the way. It read: "Warning to those with peanut allergies: crawl back out today and retreat until tomorrow." Seraphina lifted the sign and crawled under it. She could see a kid's sized *Star Wars* glass of milk and a peanut butter cookie with chocolate chips. After gobbling that up, she crawled farther down the duct work and found another plate of chocolate peanut butter chip cookies which were equally divine.

Clara's portion sizing skills were perfect. Seraphina never got too full on cookies, but always had that just right, content feeling after finishing. Plus, her knees and elbows never hurt because of the cushioned material along the way.

She slid into the office expecting to find Dewey and Clara. Instead, she found Michael sitting there, waiting with a plate of mint chip cookies—homemade, of course, no Girl Scouts here—and a book under his nose.

"Where is everyone?" asked Seraphina.

"Don't ask me," replied Michael. "He told me to get here thirty minutes ago, and I'm still waiting. Kind of annoying. Anything new with you?" he asked.

"Well, my dog died." Seraphina hadn't planned on blurting that out, but for some reason it had just come out unexpectedly.

"Oh," replied Michael, taking his nose out of his book and looking concerned. "What happened?"

"He was old. He's been part of the family since before I was born." Seraphina could feel that weird lump that felt like a marble in her throat. There was no way she was going to cry in front of Michael, but she couldn't control that lump of sadness.

"I lost my cat last year," said Michael with compassion. "She got hit by a car. We had to make her an outdoor cat because she kept peeing all over the house because she really wanted to go outside."

"I don't think my parents want any more pets, but I hope they'll change their minds," replied Seraphina, and then she immediately felt like a louse for not saying anything about his cat. But before she could, he continued.

"Totally different animal when she was out there . . . hunting, playing. We knew she wouldn't live as long, though. It sucked when she died. I wanted to bury her in the yard, but my mom said that's not how it's done. Plus, you know . . . germs."

Seraphina nodded. Why couldn't she find any words?

"We buried her collar there, though."

"Where?" asked Seraphina.

"In the yard."

"Oh. Right. That's sad about your cat," she said, her eyes watering. "He slept with me at night and sat on my lap when I did my home-work," she continued, but not too quietly because she didn't want to sound as upset as she felt inside.

"Yeah," replied Michael. "It's still so weird not having Cabbage—that was my cat's name—around now."

An awkward silence followed, and neither of them knew what to talk about next. Seraphina felt her face flush. She couldn't figure out why because she didn't feel embarrassed, really.

"Did you get the joke?" asked Michael. "Retreat?"

"Huh?" Seraphina felt totally confused.

"Before that first batch of cookies. It said to 'retreat.' Come back tomorrow. Get it? Go back and then they'll re-treat . . ."

"No, you think that was intentional?"

"Sure! Why not?"

Just then, Dewey came upstairs, and Clara came shooting down the slide. They both had a pile of books three heads high in their hands, titled things like *Dirt and Germs*; *Are We Too*

Clean?; *A Germy World Survival Guide*; *Should Parents Expose Kids to Germs?*; *Mysophobia: a Pathological Fear of Contamination and Germs*; et cetera.

"Oooof," Dewey blew out air as he set the books down on his desk. "Sorry. We've been up all night researching. We've got the plan."

"Oh, hi, Seraphina. Michael, is it OK if Seraphina's here?"

"Sure. Why not?" he replied.

It never occurred to her it might *not* be OK to be there, but she tried not to let on and just stood there, not quite sure what to do with her hands to look casual, like it wasn't an awkward moment. She folded them in front of her chest, quickly decided that wasn't right, and clasped them behind her back instead. Then they seemed to have a mind of their own, and she found them twisting her curly ponytail.

"I think, as you've likely surmised," Dewey began, "your mom was traumatized by the whole eating cat poop thing."

"Ha!" laughed Michael. "That makes two of us. These *are* confidential services, right, Dewey? I mean, I don't need the whole world knowing I ate cat doodie! Geez!"

"Of course. Always confidential!" reassured Dewey.

Seraphina was beginning to see why Dewey had asked if it was OK if she was here now and she nodded her head in agreement at the word "confidential" to show her commitment as well.

"I've done a lot of reading," Dewey continued. "We need a two-step plan. First, we have your mom face her original fear. Then, we have her work through how her fear is being acted out, 'manifested' the professionals call it. That's it."

"So what do I need to do?"

"First, my friend, you'll need this." Dewey reached into a bag on his desk and pulled out a Tootsie Roll.

"You need to relive the original scene of the

crime. Yes, that's right. You'll need to eat poop. Well, a Tootsie Roll."

"Ewwww! No way!" exclaimed Michael and Seraphina in unison.

"You've *got* to be kidding," added Michael.

"Clara. Tell them I never kid."

"He never kids," Clara said.

"Oh boy," said Michael.

"Ohh boy," said Seraphina.

Dewey pulled out a few more Tootsie Rolls of differing sizes and handed them to Michael as he went on to explain. "After your Mom's shock and complete freak out, we're going to let her down nice and easy. You're going to tell her it's OK. They're just Tootsie Rolls.

"Then, when she calms down, remind her that you survived eating the cat poo, and you'll tell her you need her to work on this whole germ thing before she kills you."

"Ironically," Michael added dryly.

"Sure. Nice touch," said Dewey. "The books

say gradual exposure is best, but you're in a hurry, so we'll just do that part fast.

"Then we move onto phase two. After she faces her original fear, it's a brainstorming session. She lists all the things she's afraid you'll get germs from—doorknobs, elevators, other kids' hands, whatever. Then she has to rank them from one to ten in terms of how scared she is of them, and what the fear is; one being she's just a bit scared that a doorbell will give you a cold, for example, while a ten is fearing you'll drink from a water fountain and get Yellow Fever. That kind of thing. Make sure she lists at least twenty things so you have enough small ones to work on first.

"Tell her to say this: 'Germs are good. They help my son's immunity.' Then you'll ask her if she agrees with that statement—do you think she will?" Dewey paused for Michael's feedback.

"Yeah. She'll agree. She's not an idiot. She's just gone psycho on me."

"Great. So from there, help her see how many

things on her list she needs to calm down about. Remind her that you're not eating poop in real life nor are you going to die from a cold. Tell her to repeat this exercise each day when she wants to tell you to avoid germs. Then report back to me in one week. Got it?"

"I think so. That was a lot of info!"

"Oh, don't worry. Clara and I are going to go over it with you step by step as you go."

"How's he supposed to do the whole eating the Tootsie Roll thing?" asked Seraphina. She was completely intrigued by just how sophisticated Dewey had become since his early days with her mom.

"Any way he'd like, as long as she walks in and thinks it's real and has enough time to freak out about it. I'd stop it short of her calling Poison Control or 911 or something to save yourself some grief. Perhaps the bathroom is your best venue if you don't want to be seen as a complete freak of nature."

"Yeah. I think I'd like to just be seen as the kid who eats his 'Tootsie Dookie' in the bathroom, not at the kitchen table, thank you very much.

"OK. I'll do it tonight. I'd like to get this over with as soon as possible."

"Great. Hey! Tootsie Roll fun fact: the guy who invented the Tootsie Roll named it after his daughter, whose nickname was Tootsie. Guess what her real name was?"

"What?" asked Michael and Seraphina on cue.

"Clara!"

That brought big laughs all around.

Then Michael picked up his Tootsie Roll and sighed, "Well, Clara. It's good to know at least you'll be there with me in spirit."

Michael Eats Tootsie Rolls

"AAAAAAAAAAAAAAAAAAAAAAAAAAAA
AAAAAAAAAAAAAAAAAAAAAAAAAAAAA
AAAAAAAAAAAAAAAAAAAAAAAAAAAAA
AAAAAAAAAAAAAAAAAAAAAAAAAAAAA
AAAAAAAAAAAAAAAAAAAAAAAAAAAAA
AAAAAAAAAAAAAAAAAAAAAAAAAAAAA
AAAAAAAAAAAAAAAAAAAAAAAAAAAAA
AAAAAAAAAAAAAAAAAAAAAAAAAAAAA
AAAAAAAAAAAAAAAAAAAAAAAAAAAAA
AAAAAAAAAAAIIIIIIIIIIIIIIIIIIIIIIIIIIIIIIIII
IIIIIIIIIIIIIIIIIIIIIIIIIIIIIIIIIIIIIIIIIIIIIIIIIIIIII

IIIIIIIIIIIIIIIIIIIIIIIIIIIIIIIIIIIIIIIIIIIIIIIIIIIIIIIII
IIIIIIIIIIIIIIIIIIIIIIIIIIIIIIIIIIIIIIIIIIIIIIIIIIIIIIIII
IIIIIIIIIIIIIIIIIIIIIIIIIIIIIIIIIIIIIIIIIIIIIIIIIIIIIIIII
IIIIIIIIIIIIIIIIIIIIIIIIIIIIIIIIIIIIIIIIIIIIIIIIIIIIIIIII
IIIIIIIIIIIIIIIIIIIIIIIIIIIIIIIIIIIIIIIIIIIIIIIIIIIIIIIII
IIIIIIIIIIIIIIIIIIIIIIIIIIIIIIIIIIIIIIIIIIIIIIIIIIIIIIIII
IIIIIIIIIIIIIIIIIIIIIIIIIIIIIIIIIEEEEEEEEEEEEE
EEEEEEEEEEEEEEEEEEEEEEEEEEEEEEEEEE
EEEEEEEEEEEEEEEEEEEEEEEEEEEEEEEEEE
EEEEEEEEEEEEEEEEEEEEEEEEEEEEEEEEEE
EEEEEEEEEEEEEEEEEEEEEEEEEEEEEEEEEE
EEEEEEEEEEEEEEEEEEEEEEEEEEEEEEEEEE
EEEEEEEEEEEEEEEEEEEEEEEEEEEEEEEEEE
EEEEEEEEEEEEEEEEEEEEEEEEEEEEEEEEEE
EEEEEEEEEEEEEEEEEEEEEEEEEEEEEEEEEE
EEEEEEEEEEEEEEEEEEEEEEEEEEEEEEEEEE
EEEEEEEEEEEEEEEEEEEEEEEEEEEEEEEEEE
EEEEEEEEEEEEEEEEEEEEEEEEEEEEEEEEEE
EEEEEEEEEEEEEEE!!!!!!!!!!!!!!!!!!!!!!!!!!!!!!!!!!!!!
!!!
!!!

!!

!!

!!

!!

!!!!!!!!!!!!!!!!!!!!!!!!!!!!!"

Everyone Out of the Pool

Texts between Michael and Seraphina:

Michael: Well if it weren't so funny it would be terrible

M: Or maybe the other way around?

Seraphina: So it went well?

M: OMG, yes

S: Highlights, pls!

M: Me sitting on tub edge, door open so

she can walk in

M: I wait almost twenty min. but . . . She enters

M: I bite down

M: She screams.

M: I take another bite, give big grin, and wipe my chin with TP!

S: No way!

S: Did she scream?

M: Out of her mind, hysterical

M: I felt kind of bad

S: So, now what?

M: She's lying down with an ice pack on her head

M: I think I killed her.

S: Go tell her

M: I did

S: Go tell her again and the plan

M: Scared!

S: It will be OK, be brave! Go!

S: Text Dewey yet?

M: No, I will

M: Cya

Texts between Michael and Dewey:

M: OK, did it

M: Wildly successful, if killing her is part of your plan

D: Great job. Don't worry if she's upset. It's part of the plan.

D: We left a plate of cookies on the porch. Go get them and bring them up to her with cup of tea. Tell the next steps.

D: One week. Hang in there.

M: Yeah, OK!

"You know," Michael said, "when I was a kid, I thought Poison Control was this tall, windowed structure with surveillance displays and radar systems. Turns out it's just an office with a bunch of phones, men, women, and a database ready with medical advice for, um, something like three million calls a year. That's not as cool as what I was picturing when I was a little kid."

"But three million calls a year? That's a lot of poison. Someone is eating a lot of Tootsie Rolls!" laughed Dewey.

A week had passed, and the three of them were debriefing in Dewey's office.

"Yeah, most of 'em are for snake bites and carbon monoxide and stuff like that. But there *were* like, almost 6,000 cases involving poop. No big surprise that most of the calls were about little kids—I don't want to think about it otherwise! And guess what? Twenty-seven of the calls this year were listed as intentional."

"What's that mean?" asked Seraphina.

"That means," Dewey chimed in, "that twenty-seven of those callers intentionally ate feces. And it wasn't a Tootsie Roll, either!"

"Ewwwww!" they all cried out in unison.

"Well, I guess you'd have to count my cat litter party as 'intentional' though right? You know how little kids are when they stock the pool with brown trout. You gotta get 'em out fast!"

"Ewwwww!" cried Seraphina again. "That's just gross."

"Twenty-seven out of 6,000 is actually a pretty good stat," claimed Dewey. "It would suggest the other 5,000 plus are getting out of the pool without tasting the floaties."

"Yeah, ha! Guess you wouldn't have been one of them!"

"That's not funny," said Michael with a half-smile, half-scowl.

"Can we please get to the matter at hand, Michael? How'd it go with your Mom?" asked Seraphina, who hadn't been brought up to speed yet.

"She screamed for about forty-five minutes, and we're going to need new kitchen dishes, but once she understood I needed to make a point, she stopped throwing the socks out of my drawer at me and we hugged. Then we cleaned up the kitchen, and she listened. Kind of. Sort of. Clara's cookies and the tea helped.

"We've been doing the whole exercise thing with ranking fears and her mantra: 'Germs are good. They help my son's immunity.' And I'd say it's working. Except . . ."

"Except what?" asked Dewey.

"Except that I don't think she's ever going to let me eat another piece of chocolate again. Got a cure for that?"

Shocking News

If there's one thing that Dewey's dad loved, it was a good game of Monopoly. That's probably because he *always* made sure he bought Park Place first. Pretty much no one else in the family ever had as much fun playing as he did, and he always had to cajole them into it.

It was a rainy Saturday afternoon, and everyone happened to be home. They were sitting ducks.

"Who's up for a game of Monopoly?"

No reply. Not even from Dewey's mom, who busied herself at the computer and tried not to look up.

"Aw, come on. Let's just play. You guys love Monopoly. It will be fun."

"Dad," explained Stephanie, "I'd love to. Really I would, but I'm right about to, um, clean my room. And Mom's been really asking me to do that lately, right, Mom?"

"Ha! Don't rope me in to your escape, missy, unless you plan on saving me in the process. And since I have no interest in cleaning your room with you . . . while I'd love, *adore*, even, for you to clean your room, no. It's not ringing any bells."

Mom smiled.

Stephanie glared.

"Dewey? You're in, right, son? Come on! I'll let you be the dog!"

"Oh, Dad. I don't want to hurt your feelings. I feel bad. You don't want to play right, right now, do you?" sighed Dewey, hoping to guilt his dad out of it. A little reverse psychology seemed like a good strategy right about now.

"Come on! It will be fun!"

Geez. Was his dad seven years old? What was wrong with him?

His little sister was only too excited to play. She was a complete nightmare to try to play any sort of organized sport with, let alone a board game.

"I want to have that fimbwe ovuw on my side, and I need some mowe houses, and I don't wike to have that money. I just want to have one dollooow, but why awe you moving youuw dog when it's my tuwn? I want twee tuuuwns . . ."

So they all played a rousing game of Monopoly. Dewey got to be the banker, at least.

Once they got going, he could admit it wasn't too terrible, though it still made him mad inside when things didn't go his way. At least he was older now and knew not to express his disappointment or cry anymore, but he still felt like throwing over the board when he was losing.

Later, after they cleaned up—they never actually managed to finish the game, since Dewey's mom had said that they had to put it away because they needed the space on the table for dinner—everyone went their own ways. Pooh Bear went to bed. Stephanie went out with her friend and their family to a movie, and Dewey went up to his room to play on his computer. His propensity to spend time alone in his room was part of what enabled him to be able to sneak off so easily to the attic to meet with his clients.

This week, though, work was slow, and Dewey actually just spent some time in his room. He wondered if it had always been this way, or maybe it had something to do with how he and Clara had messed with the air conditioning ducts, but he could hear everything his mom and dad were talking about through the air vent in his bedroom that evening.

What he heard shocked him.

Clara Cottonwood

"Well," his dad was saying, "we'll have to tell the kids sooner than later. Moving is going to be a pretty big deal for them."

What?! Did he say "moving?" Dewey felt the blood run hot to his face. He must have misheard.

"Dewey will be fine," his mom said. "He can make friends anywhere he goes. But I'm worried about Stephanie. She's been so successful at Woodbine School. She has so much invested there. Plus Pooh Bear is just starting to get speech therapy going—though I'm sure they have that in Alaska," his mother sighed.

Alaska?! Dewey's heart raced now, and he stood directly under the air vent to make sure he didn't miss a thing.

"In any case," his dad continued, "I'm just saying that summer is right around the corner, and before you know it, we'll be off. I think it's time we let them know."

Summer? This summer? Dewey's stomach actually felt sick.

"Not yet, Don. Not yet."

"It's not going to change, you know. Stalling isn't going to—oh, honey, please don't cry!"

"I'm not crying! I love a place where the state sport is dog mushing!" she gushed through her tears.

Then the phone rang, and his dad picked it up. It was Grandma. Mom pulled herself together to talk to her, and that was the end of the conversation.

Dewey sat on the edge of his bed, stunned. *Moving? Alaska? Mom sobbing?* He felt amazed by how quickly he could go from not even realizing he had a stomach or a throat to knowing those parts of his body existed. There was a knot the size of a jawbreaker in his throat, and his stomach felt like someone had turned it upside down and inside out.

He didn't even know who to tell or what to do, so he did the only sensible thing—he sat down and clicked cookies. He was up to 55 quadrillion cookies.

When Dewey awoke the next morning, he wasn't feeling very hungry—unless you could somehow call that big black pit of sorrow in his belly hunger—but somehow he knew that if he could drag himself upstairs, Clara might be able to help him feel better.

Funny how the smell of cookies had a way of

making a guy feel like he wanted cookies after all. He poured himself a glass of milk, had a plate of cookies, and rubbed Wolfie's belly for a bit while he waited for Clara to show up.

When Wolfie was a puppy, he never seemed to like belly rubs. But now, at the old age of two, he rolled over with just the slightest of prompting and opened all four legs like a time-lapse flower in full bloom.

Dewey found Wolfie soft and comforting to touch as he mindlessly thought about his problem and tried to absorb the shock of what he'd just learned. If he moved, he'd never see Wolfie again. How could this be happening? And how come no one had asked him how he felt about it?

He took a picture of Wolfie and sent it to Seraphina. #Fluffles.

When Clara slid in, she could immediately tell something was amiss.

"Sir? What's wrong?"

Wolfie bit down on his black and white skunk, gave it a shake and a toss. When no one joined in the game, he settled back into his cushion like a black and white comma, closed his eyes, and went to sleep.

Though Dewey had known Clara for all his years growing up, he probably never would have considered her for an assistant had he not run into her in the department store that one summer.

In Dewey's home, the end of the school year meant swimming, popsicles, and free time! But it also signaled his mother to purge their drawers and closets, which meant Dewey had to stand in the middle of his room trying on pants, shorts, shirts, bathing trunks, pajamas—everything!—until his mother had finished making piles of things she would send to his little cousin, box up for Pooh Bear, or put back in his drawers.

That's how summers began. And summers ended with the family taking a trip to the department store to fill in the missing gaps. Dewey had no idea Clara even worked in a department store, and he was in the middle of complaining to his mother when Clara saved the day.

"Why can't you just order them online like a normal mother?" whined Dewey.

"What? And miss out on this special time together? Not on your life, mister."

Uugh. He stood in the dressing room trying on some pants. This, in his opinion, remained the *only* thing worse than having to try on clothes at home. Dewey looked at himself in the wall-to-wall mirrors. He looked kind of pale, and his arms were too skinny.

He came out to show his mom the third pair of corduroy pants. The other two, which he thought fit just right, his mom felt wouldn't leave "enough room to grow."

"Okay?" he asked, with just a bit too much attitude.

"Okay?!" replied a little old lady. "Well, I'd say

that they're more than okay. Those pants on that bottom is what I'd call a real lady catcher!"

Dewey had looked around for his mom at that moment. And then looked behind and around him to be sure that this old lady was really talking to him. He did a double take and realized it was their longtime family friend and babysitter Clara Cottonwood!

"Now come here so I can fix them up a bit." She led Dewey to the middle of the dressing room like she worked there, and cuffed his pants a bit so they weren't too long and untucked his shirt.

"You don't want to look like some sort of dweeb with your shirt tucked in," she added, and gave a wink.

What's Clara doing here? And where did my mom go? Dewey had wondered.

As if she could read his mind, Clara straightened his shirt and added, "Your mom is out at the clothing area looking for socks for you. Can I get you a shirt that I think would *really* make that outfit blue chip?"

"Um, sure," replied Dewey.

Why, he wondered, *wasn't it Dad's idea of a good time to take him shopping?* This would be a whole lot less painful. Firstly, they'd be in and out in about ten minutes. Secondly . . . well, secondly, there'd be no secondly because his dad hated to shop as much as he did, and they'd be out eating pizza instead.

Clara returned with a big pile of shirts.

Much to Dewey's surprise, the shirts actually looked pretty good. She'd brought him a red shirt with a sky high tower, one with some stick figure kid skateboarding, a shirt with one of his favorite computer game figures, and a plain, inoffensive, light blue one. He didn't even know department stores had shirts like these.

"Oh," he said surprised. "These are actually pretty okay."

His mom returned and told him to come out

and "model" each one of the outfits.

In the privacy of his dressing room, he had to admit, he looked pretty good in the first one he put on. He didn't look so pale or scrawny after all.

"Oh, I like it!" his mom said as he came out to show her and gave Clara a hug hello. Clara gave a nod, and he went back in to try on the next one. Clara handed him some long shorts, which she called "deck pants," instead of the corduroys his mother had chosen, reasoning that the fall weather is often warmer than the summer months and suggested getting the corduroy pants for the winter.

Dewey went back into the dressing room and got dressed. He was actually pretty pleased with the new clothes, and not too annoyed about the time he'd invested in getting them.

Months passed, but when Dewey opened his new office and started to get so busy it was obvious he needed an assistant to help run things, kind of to his own surprise, Clara Cottonwood immediately came to mind. Now that he was getting older, he didn't go over as often to her house for babysitting as he used to, so when he spotted her walking a new dog while he and Colin played hide and seek tag in the park, he took a time-out to go greet the puppy and approach her about the topic.

There were "No Dogs Allowed" signs posted all around the park. Clara Cottonwood felt that those rules were made for folks who didn't clean up after their dogs, and since she knew she always cleaned up after her dog, and even other people's sometimes for that matter, it was just fine if she broke that particular regulation.

Dewey greeted her and asked all about Wolfie. She had been talking about getting a puppy for years.

"You did it! You got a new dog! He's really cute!" he'd said as Wolfie brought out that now infamous pink tongue and licked, licked, licked Dewey's chin. "What kind is he?"

"A Havanese—the national dog of Cuba! Their ancestors were raised to be lap dogs hundreds of years ago."

His plumed, little tail curled over his small rump, and he ran in circles.

Colin, who realized that Dewey was no longer seeking him, had come out of hiding to see what was going on.

"Hello," said Colin, stooping down to also pet Wolfie, who immediately jumped up and wagged his tail.

"Off, boy," admonished Clara. "No jumping."

"What the narwhal, he feels like a rabbit!" Colin said once he could catch Wolfie in his hands again.

Dewey stood and tried to figure out the best way to broach the subject of employment with her.

"Have you named him yet? He's so soft. You should call him Narwhal," Colin said while petting him and looking up at Clara.

"OK, that makes no sense," said Dewey.

Clara chuckled. "Not 'Narwhal.' 'Wolfie.' Just wait until you feel how sharp his teeth are. He's a hunter with a toy skunk, alright. Needed a more ferocious name."

Colin and Dewey looked at that little black and white ball of fluff and laughed. He looked a lot more like a baby panda bear than a wolf! But then again, he didn't look much like a whale with a uni-horn either so "Wolfie" certainly made as much sense as "Narwhal." Dewey was just about to say so to Colin, but he could see that Clara was getting ready to go, so he just blurted out, "I have this business, see."

Clara and Wolfie cocked their heads sideways with interest, and Dewey felt encouraged to continue.

"I kind of help kids solve problems they have with their parents. And I could really use an assistant because, well, it just seems like there are *a lot* of difficult parents out there! The paperwork is killing me. I'm still a kid in school, ya know? And it's just too much for me to handle alone. Would you possibly be interested?"

Was she ever. Her position at the department store was over, having only been temporary for the seasonal sale, and Clara welcomed the companionship the job offered. At first, it was pretty part-time. As Dewey became busier, her cookie baking became more central to their operation, and Clara became an integral part of the business.

And now, after all they'd been through, they were about to lose it all. Dewey didn't know how to tell Clara, even though she'd be the one who would understand the most.

Physician, Heal Thyself

Dewey told Seraphina his secret first instead.

She put her arm around him, and he felt the blood from his shoulders rush to his cheeks.

"I'll meet you at your place after dinner, and we'll tell Clara together. Then we'll figure it out. Don't worry. Something will give."

But Seraphina wasn't so sure. She felt a little lump of sadness in her throat and behind her eyes at the thought of Dewey actually leaving for good.

After all they'd been through, Dewey decided

he needed to tell Clara himself, so he asked her to meet him a bit earlier than he expected Seraphina to show up.

So, here she was now, looking directly at him and asking him what was wrong. He didn't know how he was going to tell her.

"Clara," he blurted out, "I overheard my parents say we are moving to Alaska this summer for my dad's work."

There. He'd said it.

"Hmmm. That's bad," she said as if it were any other bit of news. "I need to grab some paperwork off my desk," she muttered as she headed over to it and busied herself. "Oh, there it is."

Dewey felt confused by her response. Hadn't she heard him? "Clara. Did you hear what I said?"

"I heard you, Boss. Hang on one second. I need to print something."

Dewey was shocked. After all they'd been through. No tears? No upset?

Clara handed him a piece of paper and a pen and led him to sit down on the cushion opposite his desk where his clients usually sat.

"Here," she said. "Fill this out, please."

It was their client information form.

"Aw, come on, Clara. What are you doing?" Dewey complained.

Just then, Seraphina came sliding into the room.

"Sorry. Am I late? Is it my fault she plants little cookie stops along the way to distract me?"

"No. You're not late. Just in time to help me understand *what the fruit* Clara is doing."

"Sir, please. The paperwork."

"This is dumb, Clara."

"Indulge me, sir."

So, Dewey filled it out:

Name: Dewey Fairchild

Grade: 5th

School: Franklin Elementary

"Do I *really* need to fill in my address, Clara?"

"Sir, please. The entire form," insisted Clara.

Seraphina just sat down next to Wolfie and stroked him and watched with great curiosity.

> Home Address: 5555 Franklin Way
>
> Best Entry to Your Home Without Being Noticed:

"Ha! The attic," he laughed. "OK, sorry. Laundry room door?" he scribbled that down instead.

> Top Three Hiding/Observing Places in Your Home: living room closet, behind the couch in family room, under my bed
>
> Siblings (names and ages): Stephanie-fourteen, Pooh Bear-five
>
> Pets: just Wolfie ☺
>
> Parents' Names: Karen and Don Fairchild
>
> Problem Parent(s) Cause You: They have to move. Don't know why—has to do with my dad's job.

Dewey let out a big sigh. "Happy now?"

"Yes," replied Clara. "Because now I know you aren't moving."

"Oh yeah? And why is that?" asked Dewey, half-amused and half-annoyed.

"Because this is what you do! This is what *we* do! We solve parent problems. Now this kid Dewey and his parents have a big problem. Let's get to it."

"Oh yay!" exclaimed Seraphina and clapped her hands together.

"Hmmm," said Dewey.

Dewey Picks a Tough Case

It would be nice if the world revolved around him right now, but unfortunately, while Dewey was hiding out under his bed, trying to gather information about why his father's job was making them move, Clara still had a backlog of client cases for him to solve.

Tommy's mom yells too much; Georgina's dad picks his nose in public; Ken's parents force him to play the piano and practice all the time. Dewey had promised poor Georgina he'd pick her case first. "Get it, Clara?! I'm *picking* her case first!"

Dewey amused himself, but he had to admit, having a public nose picker for a father pretty much nosed ahead of other people's problems.

When he finally got around to her paperwork, he saw it wasn't just about nose-picking but also loud public burping.

"He thinks just because he says 'excuse me' that it's OK to burp like that. I don't think he really realizes when he's picking his nose though," Georgina clarified when they met.

Having Georgina as a client represented just how far-reaching Dewey's reputation had spread. Georgina attended a private school down the street from where Dewey and his friends attended school. She wasn't a stranger to them, as they'd all been together on the preschool circuit, but it had been years.

"I think we should tackle one issue at a time here," began Dewey. "Let's start with the belching, and then we'll move on to the nose picking." Somehow, that felt more doable.

Georgina began to squirm a bit in her cushion, blushing at the mention of the nose picking.

Clara keyed right into her discomfort and took the opportunity to pass around her newest invention: cookie dough cookies. They were baked cookies with chunks of cookie dough in them.

She had two varieties, crunchy and chewy, and since these were prototypes, she handed out both and asked Dewey and Georgina's opinions. This distraction, Clara reasoned, would help take some pressure off of poor Georgina as she answered the tough questions.

"So, what kinds of places or situations does he tend to burp?" asked Dewey.

"Cookie?" asked Clara.

"Yes, please. Thank you. Well, I guess for sure at our kitchen table. And that always makes my mom mad. My brother seems to think it's funny, but I hate it too."

"Where else?" asked Dewey, taking notes.

"Well, he'll also do it at a restaurant, which is bad because people turn in their seats and look. Or, say, at a baseball game. Or wherever there's food, really. He eats, he burps. He drinks, he burps. And they are loud! And long ones! It's really bad. Sometimes they even, um, smell." She wriggled around in her seat again.

"How did you enjoy that cookie?" asked Clara. "That was the crunchy one. I'm going to get you the chewy ones soon, but they have to come out of the oven."

"OK . . . and now, the nose picking?" continued Dewey.

"Uugh. It's the worst. He doesn't seem to realize he's doing it. It's always while he has some faraway look on his face, and then, before you know it, he is working his fat finger into that hole like . . . like . . . like Winnie the Pooh trying wriggle himself into Rabbit's hole for honey." Georgina voice got bizarrely loud as she said "for honey," as if she were yelling it across the room.

"Hey, that's funny! Pooh Bear is my sister's name. Well, nickname."

"What? Really! That's really weird. Sorry! No offense intended," Georgina reddened.

"Ha! None taken," Dewey reassured. "So, when would you say this excavation most often occurs?" asked Dewey, scribbling as quickly as he could in his notebook.

"Well, let's see. Driving. Watching TV or out at a movie. Sometimes, if my grandma starts going on and on about something, he'll just start up then, too."

"Now I know this last bit of information may seem graphic and insensitive, and I am sorry in advance, but if you can tell me, it will save a lot of stakeout time and let us get started a lot quicker. Do you know what he *does* with the boogers? I mean, he doesn't eat them, does he?"

"The chewy cookies are hot out of the oven and ready for you to try!" sang Clara with delight, handing them each a small plate with two cookie dough cookies on it and a mini glass of cold milk.

Dewey rolled his eyes. *Timing, Clara! Timing!*

In fact, the timing proved to be good and so did the cookies. They both agreed that they liked the cookie dough chunks in the crunchy cookie better.

Georgina admitted that she didn't know *what* her dad did with the boogers, because as soon as his finger started doing its crawl, she looked the other way. But she sure feared that others did not, and that's why she'd come for help—that, and because their dinner table sounded a lot like a beached elephant seal sat with them.

Dewey shook Georgina's hand and then so did Clara.

"Don't worry, Georgina. We'll crack this case, or my name isn't Dewey Fairchild," and out Georgina went the way she came, a little more hopeful and a lot more satiated.

Clara looked over at Dewey and gave him

a wink. "Boogers and burps, eh? Well, eat slugs! This case ought to be fun, Boss."

"Yeah. You sure can pick 'em, Clara," he wise-cracked as he walked out.

"Ah ha ha ha ha ha! Oh, pick 'em. Yeah. I get it. Pick 'em!"

Wolfie just rolled over for a belly rub, and if she wasn't mistaken, let out a "BUUURRRP."

A Nickel for Your Thoughts

Under his bed was an excellent spot to gather new information from his parents. Dewey's bedroom was next to the kitchen, where conversations between his parents often occurred, and, as he'd already learned, he could also hear a lot coming through the vent when they were in the living room.

His parents were in the kitchen husking and chopping up tomatillos for some sort of white bean chili recipe his dad wanted to try, which Dewey would never consider eating.

It made no sense to Dewey that they were moving. His dad and Dr. Bernard had worked together in the dentist practice as long as Dewey could remember. Surely he didn't *want* to go to Alaska?

"Look, Karen. I don't love the idea of Alaska any more than you do. But this is my chance to finally get out from under his thumb—really make it mine, you know? And Alaska is beautiful. It will be an adventure. Clean air. The Northern Lights. Bears! Eagles! Whales!"

"But, Don. That's a vacation, not our home. I know this is a tremendous opportunity, and you've been frustrated to say the least, but are you so unhappy with how things are that you'd really relocate us all to Alaska?"

"What awe you doing, Dewey?" Dewey felt hot breath on his face. Pooh Bear had climbed under the bed with him and whispered so loudly in his face that she might as well have spoken it aloud.

"Nothing. I lost something. I was looking for it."

"I couwd hewp, Dewey. What did you wooze?"

"I wost . . . Argh! I *lost* a nickel. See it anywhere?"

Pooh Bear looked all over beneath his bed and found a pencil eraser and a marble he really liked and was glad to have back.

"Thanks," he said. "That's OK. I have another nickel."

"I have a nickew in my woom. You couwd use it if you give it back," and she ran out to go get it for him. *She really can be kind of sweet,* he reflected, *when she isn't bugging the bajeepers out of me.*

Shoot. She'd only be gone for a few minutes and Dewey needed time to think. He hadn't gotten a lot of helpful information. He had recorded it though, so at least he could replay it later and see if he'd missed anything that might be helpful.

Right now he needed to get back to work on Georgina's case. He hoped Pooh Bear would side-track herself along the way. He really didn't have time to hang out with her now. He climbed out from under the bed.

"Deewweyyy. I think I have a nickew," she said, and she proceeded to dump coins from a jar the size of her head all over his bed, and began to dig through them.

"Hewe you go!" she said, handing him a quarter.

"Thanks," said Dewey. He dug out two dimes from her pile and handed them back to her.

"Here's your change."

Rhinotillexomania

So, Georgina's dad was what you'd call a real nose picker, alright.

Dewey followed him around for a few days and all the stuff Dewey had been taught as a kid to stop doing—belching, yawning loudly, and sure, he'd admit it, nose picking—this guy dished them out like a preschooler during story time.

From his spot in the closet, Dewey had a clear view of Georgina's dad at his desk. First there was the sideways thumb pick. Dewey spied him in front of the computer with his thick left thumb up the side of his left nostril. As his right hand rested on the mouse and flipped through the day's news stories, the left thumb, supported by the pointer and middle fingers against the side of his nose and his cheek, would start its work—up to the top and slide down . . . up to the top and slide down . . . up to the, ah! Got one. Pull, pull, pull with the left thumb until he'd slid out his morsel. Then he would mindlessly roll and roll it and . . . drop it onto the carpet.

He'd go back again until he'd made an entire sweep of his left nostril and then, crossing his left arm over to his right nostril, continue to work the mouse with his right hand and sweep the sides of his right nostril for boogers.

Dewey noted he'd stop his "work" if the phone rang or someone came in. But then he'd go right back to it.

Georgina's dad punctuated the end of each nose picking session by a pinch to his nostrils with his thumb and forefinger three times, and then he'd rub under his nose with his pointer finger.

It went the same way each and every time he sat down in front of a computer or television—he'd sit down and, bam, reach for the stars. Dewey took extra care to wipe the bottom of his shoes before going back in his own home.

Car rides had an entirely different style of picking. Dewey discovered this by actually following him to work. Clara sat on four pillows to make herself tall enough to reach the steering wheel of her Buick station wagon. The dashboard was covered in toy frogs she'd collected, which had attached themselves from years in the sun.

She wore big sunglasses—each lens was the size of the magnifying glass in Dewey's science kit. She looked like some sort of alien-fly-bug creature, but she had been riding in cars almost since the advent of them, and she knew how to handle the road . . . even in a station wagon!

Dewey held onto his hat as they hit the curves

and sat in the back, slouched down in his seat with his own dark glasses on and his notebook out, observing Georgina's dad.

"Look at that, Clara. The car ride pick is a full finger insert," he commented as he attempted to take notes while the car bumped along. "More of an excavation than a sweep. Looks to be some wet stuff along with the boogers he's, eww, great! Rolling up it in little balls for a while—wait, I'm starting the clock—before actually setting them free on the highway," he narrated from the back seat. "Three minutes on that one!"

"Get over a lane, would ya, Clara? I need some cars between us for cover."

Dewey put his binoculars up to his eyes just in time to catch Georgina's dad wiping lingering snot from his fingers onto a tissue in a nearby Kleenex box. As far as Dewey could tell, though, Georgina's dad didn't actually remove the tissue from the box, but instead just wiped it on the one still in there. Dewey made a mental note to never use tissues at Georgina's house.

When he got home at the end of the day, that man was still at his picking. Dewey wondered how on earth one man could actually produce so many nuggets to pick.

"Eww! Nuggets?" Seraphina cried when he reported his findings so far.

"I'm sorry," Dewey feigned a formal, nerdy voice. "I should have said 'dried up nasal mucus.'"

"Not helping!"

"You're too picky."

"Ha!"

"Seriously. Don't be a snot bag about this. I need help."

"Dewey!"

"OK, OK. I'll snot. I mean stop!"

Seraphina was laughing as Clara came in with a fresh batch of what looked like brownies.

"Brownies?" asked Dewey in surprise.

"Yes, I decided to try something bar shaped for a change. Do you approve?"

"This is higghly irreeeglrar," he glugged, his mouth full of brownie and milk.

But he went back for more, so Clara took that as an affirmative and went back to her baking. If these went over well, she planned on doing the next batch with Tootsie Rolls as the chocolate base, though that probably meant poor Michael would never try one!

"So, next steps?" asked Seraphina as she reached for another brownie.

"Honestly, this one has me a bit stumped. I think I'll let it percolate a bit and move on to his burping and see where that takes me. He yawns really loudly, too, sometimes—like, too loudly. Georgina didn't mention it, but I think it might be part of the picture here.

"Anyway, he seems like a nice enough guy. Just some advice for you. If you go over to Georgina's house, I'd keep your shoes and socks on."

"Why?" asked Seraphina.

"Can't really say more. Client confidentiality

and all. Just trust me on this one."

"OK," she replied. "Any updates on your life?"

"Nope. Last I heard we're set to move to Alaska this summer and nothing, not even my mother, the person who gets cold when the temperature drops below seventy degrees, is going to be able to stop it from happening."

Dewey stayed up late that evening replaying the tape of his parents' conversation and making some notes.

+ Dad wants to go, not Mom

+ Mom said Dad "unhappy"

+ Also said "frustrated"

+ Dad said "get out from under thumb"

Why is Dad frustrated? Whose thumb? What's in Alaska?

Dewey felt like throwing over the chair in

his room. Why did Pooh Bear have to come in and interrupt? How was he going to get the answers to these questions? He needed to think like Dewey, the parent-problem solver, not like the client. He sat down in the chair and put his face in his hands. Then he took out the sheet he'd filled out for Clara and tried to look at it as if he were Dewey Fairchild, PPS, not the guy whose parents were causing him problems.

OK. Step one: he needed to follow Dad around at work and see what was going on there. But how could he go unnoticed? He couldn't. He wished he could just bug him with some spy device. Wait. He couldn't go, but maybe Seraphina could! He'd send her in as a dental patient and have her spy for him. Maybe Colin, too.

Yes! That could maybe work as a start. With that idea he could finally breathe easier and head off to bed without too much tossing and turning.

The whole thing seemed so unreal. He wasn't really sure what to do, but at least he felt like he'd be trying to do something now.

Dewey spent the following days observing Georgina's dad's behavior. As Georgina reported, he burped loudly after meals. She'd mentioned he sounded a good deal like an elephant seal, but hearing was believing. It was as if his whole stomach churned and echoed with a megaphone in his throat, and the noise slapped and flapped and roared.

He yawned almost as loudly and at inopportune times.

His wife was right in the middle of telling him about her day when a big one came on.

"So the thing that upset me the most about what Harriet said to me, and the reason I broke down and cried then and there was—"

YYAWWWWNNNN, Georgina's dad's mouth opened so widely, Dewey could have sworn it had hinges that must have come undone.

"Todd!" cried Georgina's mother as she ran out of the room crying.

"What just happened?" Georgina's dad asked Georgina and her brother. He seemed genuinely confused. They just went back to their macaroni and cheese. He finished his and belched.

"So all of this is pretty standard in your house?" Dewey asked Georgina, reviewing all that he'd observed over the last few days.

"Yep. I'd say that sums it up," said Georgina, munching on a brownie with a sugar cookie layer in the middle. "Mmm! Interesting," she added, nodding after she saw Clara looking for approval.

"Huh," said Dewey. "Well, I suppose I have enough data to go on. I think we can assume he does this outside of the home as well . . . we know he does it in his car. Let me get back to you on the next steps. I want to do a bit more research. I have a hunch, but I want to see if it pans out."

When Georgina left, he went to his desk to sit down and do just that. He still had a bit of time before Seraphina was due to arrive. He'd asked her to tell Colin to come, if he could, as well.

Wolfie had just returned from getting a haircut. Now, instead of looking like a small, plump sheep dog, he looked more like a frisky puppy. His fur, already soft before, now felt as soft as a mink coat, and Dewey really hoped he'd be willing to sit on his lap for a while.

At eighteen pounds, Wolfie was kind of big for the average-sized person's lap. Plus, he really didn't like to sit on a lap much, except when he was in the car, and it was moving.

Dewey wanted warm, soft inspiration though, so he hoisted Wolfie up and rubbed under his chin, hoping he could con him into staying, if only for a bit.

So far, so good.

Yawning, boogers, and burps. As he cross-referenced these it didn't take long to realize that one thing these three things had in common was breathing. And Dewey was starting to wonder if somehow that might help his case. Yawning was about opening one's mouth and taking in a long breath of air. It was an involuntary act and usually a result of being weary or drowsy, said the research.

Hey, it says here that contagious yawning can happen with dogs. Dewey tried yawning at Wolfie to see if he'd yawn as well. Nope. Nothing.

After Seraphina and Colin left, Dewey spent hours, late into the night, on the computer researching the causes of yawning, burping, and boogery noses.

All roads had led to one conclusion.

"Your dad's not an inconsiderate lout," Dewey shared with Georgina the next day in his office. "I think he has a medical condition called Rhinotillexomania or something like it, and needs help."

Georgina's eyes got as big and round as Clara's cookies.

"Oh, no. Don't worry!" assured Dewey. "I don't think it's anything serious. He could have allergies, or an acid reflux problem. Or both! A trip or two to a specialist though, and you will all be much better off, I'm sure of it."

Georgina left, relieved and assuring Dewey that she'd be encouraging her dad to see someone in the next few days.

It had grown late again. He had figured out what to do for Georgina. Why couldn't he do the same for his own family?

He scooped up Wolfie, who'd been sleeping in his bed, and put him on his lap. Wolfie yawned. So did Dewey.

Dr. Don Fairchild, DDS

Dewey's dad and his fellow dentist had their office downtown in a charming, older one-story brick building. It looked more like a house than a dentist's office, and his dad liked that because he felt like it would make his patients feel more comfortable.

Truthfully, Dewey didn't think it mattered much. Going to the dentist wasn't really on anybody's hit parade, but at least they had a bubble gum machine filled with little toys for the kids at the end.

His dad's boss, Dr. Bernard, had owned the practice for thirty years and hired Dewey's dad to work with him. Dewey had always liked Dr. Bernard. He talked to kids like they were adults, not kids, and he let you push all of the buttons to make the chair go up and fill the cup with water.

It was a bit more complicated than Dewey had anticipated to get his friends into the office. It turns out you can't just make an appointment if you're a kid, there's a bunch of insurance forms and stuff, and they kind of expect an adult to at least walk in with you.

The workaround for Seraphina had been her idea. She called the office as a student saying that she wanted to observe and interview a dentist for career day. Her plan was to interview Dewey's dad and try to find out anything that might help them. Meanwhile, Colin, who was long overdue for a checkup anyway, would ask his dad if Clara could take him to the dentist. Then he could pump Dr. Bernard for all the information he could get while he made "small talk."

"I hope you know how much you're gonna owe me after this, Dewey. I've been steering clear of the dentist for three years now."

"Three years? How've you done that?"

"Well, my mom thinks my dad has brought me. My dad thinks my mom has. I was hoping to keep this up for at least a few more years."

"Your teeth are going to fall out of your head!" laughed Dewey.

"I'll take my chances," Colin said with his lips covering his teeth so it looked like he didn't have any. "I *hate* the dentist."

When they got to Colin's house, they found Colin's dad doing some work on his computer.

"Dad, can I show you something?" Colin scraped his fingernail against his tooth and showed his father the resulting layer of thick greenish-white gunk under his nail.

"Colin! That's vile!" his dad replied. "You need your teeth cleaned!"

"Pre-cisely!" uttered Colin with as much enthusiasm as a friend who was trying to save another friend from moving to Alaska could muster under such circumstances.

Then Dewey and Colin asked Colin's dad if Clara could take him to the dentist.

Colin's dad agreed without any difficulty, but said he'd take him himself.

Colin scraped another tooth and when Colin's dad looked sufficiently grossed out, Dewey dialed the phone to his dad's office.

"Hi! This is Dewey. I have a good friend who really needs his teeth cleaned soon. Seriously. Like tomorrow. They are growing algae or baby caterpillars or something on them—" Colin shot him a *Hey! What's-the-big-idea?* look but Dewey continued, "Can you speak to dad and fit him in somewhere tomorrow? I know dad said his day was really full, but maybe Dr. B?"

"Yes, I'm sure they'd be fine seeing Dr. Bernard," he continued, looking at Colin's dad for approval.

Colin scraped another tooth and wiped it on his jeans for added effect.

Colin's dad nodded his head a firm yes, and put out his hand for the phone. He set up the appointment.

So, there they were now. Seraphina in one room, interviewing and observing. Colin in the chair. There remained only the one small problem of getting rid of Colin's dad, which, as of go-time, they still hadn't quite figured out, so he was in the waiting room catching up on emails on his phone.

"Hey there, Colin, is it?" said Dr. Bernard. "How are things in your mouth these days?"

"Fine, sir." In fact, this was the first teeth cleaning his mouth would have in three years, and coming here today was a complete testament to his friendship for Dewey. He was *freaking out* inside! Colin hoped Dr. Bernard wouldn't notice.

"Go ahead and fill up that cup right there by

pushing that button."

"Ah, good looking set of teeth you've got there, son. That one's coming out soon. Been losing them steadily, I see. I do see a bit of plaque buildup. We'll take care of that, no worries."

As he sat there, Colin began thinking about narwhals and their single, gigantic tooth. Sometimes it got up to ten feet long! Talk about a lot of plaque build-up. Did they have narwhal dentists half a mile down on the dark ocean floor?

Meanwhile, Seraphina sat with the hygienist asking questions and taking notes. The office manager had said that Dr. Fairchild's busy day had just gotten even busier, due to a walk-in emergency first thing in the morning. Someone had the bright idea of trying to pull their kid's tooth out using a doorknob and a string, and it hadn't gone so well. Now he was running very behind. So she suggested Seraphina talk to the hygienist instead.

Seraphina filled her notebook with a bunch of

useless information about how the hygienist went into the dentistry profession because of how she'd had a toothache as a child.

When she finally got to go in and at least observe Dewey's dad, he was filling the tooth of some old guy Seraphina had met in the waiting room earlier. He had arrived an hour early for his appointment because he didn't like to run late. He was a short little man, and his feet hardly reached the end of the chair. He looked like a duck in his little, green suit, with his big bill open wide and his feet fanned out on the chair.

"Seraphina! Lovely to see you and your teeth today!" cried Dewey's dad.

"Thank you, Dr. Fairchild," she blushed and smiled.

"Oh, don't be silly. Call me Don. You're Dewey's friend! I'll bet your teeth are in immaculate condition. Let us have a looksee."

She smiled from across the room where she sat on a little round stool.

"Oh, very nice!" he replied, and went back to his drilling as she took more notes in her book.

Meanwhile, two doors down, Colin's mouth wasn't quite as impressive as Seraphina's, and this undercover operation was about to take an unfortunate turn for the worse.

"I don't like the look of that lateral incisor. I'll get a quick picture of it, but we probably need to fill it," said Dr. Bernard cheerfully.

Colin's mind quickly swam up from under the sea.

"Um. What? Today?"

"Sure. Today's as good a day as any, and I don't want that small hole that's growing to swallow your head."

Colin gulped.

"I'll just check in with your dad, and we'll get started."

Colin's dad stuck his head in the room.

"You doing OK, son?"

Colin nodded yes, though he was far from

sure about that at all.

"Great. Well, you're in great hands, but this may take a bit. You good with me going back to work?"

Colin, who couldn't answer, just kept staring at his dad as he spoke.

"I ran into your friend Seraphina. Did you know she's here doing something for school? Anyway, she said they could drive you home. So I'll check you out and meet you back home. I can work from home actually, so when you get there I'll be waiting, but I really didn't plan on this day, and I've got to get back to some calls. You good with that, son?"

Well, Seraphina seemed to have it all worked out, didn't she? he thought. *Everything except that big drill about to put a hole in my head!*

He gave his dad a thumbs-up for him to leave, relieved that at least part of the plan was falling into place. He closed his eyes for a moment, wishing he were the one gathering information for "career day."

Then, before he knew what happened, little cardboard pieces were stuck in his mouth for x-rays, and they were prepping him for Novocain—not to fill the tooth, but to pull it right out!

"You see here, Colin?" said Dr. Bernard holding up the x-ray to the light over Colin's head. "Right here is your tooth. And this right here is the handy work of a Snickers. As I told your dad, no point in filling a hole that big. Eat more carrots and apples, and brush and floss better, so your teeth stay in your head, and the only hole in your mouth is your mouth."

And with that, he rubbed some bitter tasting numbing gel on the inside of Colin's cheek and went to work on him. Colin tried to distract himself by picturing Dr. Bernard removing one of those ten-foot-long narwhal tusks.

"Yooouusjh ttrrruuuyyyy thssss . . . drrr-roooolllllll."

He'd wanted to tell Dr. Bernard he should try this out on a narwhal sometime, but the words didn't come. His mouthful of gauze made it impossible for him to talk. How was he going to ask him questions now and do his undercover work for Dewey?

There was what felt like a few tugs in his mouth, and then Dr. Bernard put down his little pliers on the table near Colin's face and slid it away.

"You're all done, son. Nothing in your mouth now but good, clean, healthy teeth. Bite down gently now on this piece of gauze. That's it. Let the Novocain wear off before you attempt to eat so you don't bite your tongue or lip. You'll be numb for a bit. Sit here a few minutes, and we'll set you free," and out walked Dr. Bernard, patting Colin on the head as he headed for his next unsuspecting mouth.

What? There wasn't any gauze packing his mouth? But his mouth felt full. He picked up the little mirror on the tray and looked. Other than the hole where the tooth used to be, his mouth appeared the same, but when he tried to move it, nothing followed his command. He tried to smile. Nope. Pucker his lips. Oops. Drool. He poked at his lip gently. It felt like raw chicken. Weird.

Seraphina glanced in the room and saw that they had trouble. Big trouble. This mission appeared doomed before it had taken off. Dewey would be so disappointed in them. But what could she do?

"What happened?" she cried.

"I bldon't blknow!" Colin tried to say but his lips and tongue were thick and numb.

"I bl-ink—" but then he just drooled, and Seraphina jumped in and said, "Please! Don't try to talk!" She handed him a tissue. "Let me think."

She gazed out the window and felt like a total failure. After all Dewey had done for her, they were going to lose him to Alaska because they couldn't handle one stupid assignment. She had totally failed in getting any information out of Dewey's dad. He didn't have time to talk with her at all! Colin had been totally useless gathering any information.

Then, out of nowhere, Seraphina suddenly had an idea. And out of sheer desperation, she ran with it.

"May I use your restroom?" she asked the woman at the front desk.

Seraphina snuck off behind the bathroom into one of the patient rooms. And then another, and finally a third. There, she found what definitely looked to her like the fuse box. She opened the little metal door, and it looked just like the one they had at home. It was a bunch of light switches, some labeled and others not.

There was no time to read the labels, and besides, she felt too nervous. She looked over her shoulder, took a deep breath, and flipped each and every switch the other direction, praying she wouldn't die of an electrical shock or blow up the building or something.

Flip, flip—she could hear people starting to make a commotion now. It was working. The lights went off in the room she stood in. She just kept flipping as fast as she could. The switches were stiff and hard to flip and little dents formed in her fingertips, but she did them all. She closed the door and looked around for something to slide in front of it. There wasn't anything tall enough though, so she peered around the corner into the room next to her and saw a bookcase.

Too heavy. And too obvious, anyway. Oh! The plant! It was the perfect height. But it was too heavy. Too much time had passed. She slipped into the bathroom and closed the door which turned out to be a big mistake because it was pitch black in there as soon as the door closed.

"Ack!" she cried out. It wasn't logical, but something inside of her panicked that the door could now be locked, and she'd be stuck in the dark bathroom alone.

She put both hands out in front of her and felt for the door and the handle. To her great relief, it turned in her hand. She looked both ways and headed back out to Colin, using some of the natural light that crept through a few of the office windows to guide her.

Colin had been sitting in the chair, waiting for his tongue to stop feeling like a brick, when the power had gone down.

Naww. Couldn't be, he had thought.

But it was. Seraphina quietly came in and startled him when she touched his shoulder from behind the dentist chair.

"Now, Mr. Truly Drooly," she whispered, "you've *got* to pull yourself together. We have to divide up and just listen—listen to *anything* that we might overhear that could be helpful to Dewey. 'Cause, so far, all we've got are excessively clean teeth and your cow tongue, and somehow I don't think we're going to impress Dewey much with that. You can handle listening right now, can't you?"

Colin looked hurt, but nodded and slid out of his chair.

"You go stake out the front staff area to see what they're talking about. I'll go see what the doctors have to say. We've probably got a good thirty minutes until they realize that I tripped the switches, if you help me move this plant over there in front of the fuse box.

"We won't try to leave together. When you can talk without biting your cheek, we'll compare notes later. Good?"

They slipped into the hallway, and Seraphina pointed to Colin where the plant needed to go. Evidently though, Colin's tongue must have really felt longer than usual because he tripped on it and went flying down the hallway—that or he tripped on his own feet. Whatever the cause, the fall made a huge noise, and Seraphina ran to catch up to him and slid him into a patient room and closed the door behind them.

She looked down at him, put her finger in front of her mouth to signal that he should only talk under penalty of death just as they heard people coming down the hall to see what the commotion was all about.

"I think it came from over here," someone said.

"Quick," whispered Seraphina. "In here!" She opened what looked like a small storage closet. "Don't make a sound," she mouthed.

She could hear the sound of heels walking down the hallway and voices getting closer.

Sitting still wasn't one of Colin's best skills, though, and within a minute he'd found a box filled with toys to refill the gumball dispenser, and he began opening up the little plastic bubbles to see what prizes were in each one.

"Haven't you caused enough problems, already?" She glared at him.

"But blook!" he smiled, "blere's a 'Bly BLittle

Blony' and a blittle blinature diver."

The door opened to the room they were in and Colin shut up.

"I think everyone has gone," said one voice.

"We'll have to bill the ones who didn't check out, I guess. Want to fill up the dispenser while we're here?" said another, and both kids stiffened and tried to flatten themselves as thin as possible by sucking in their breath.

The knob on the closet door started to turn.

"Nah. Let's do that tomorrow. We get a reprieve today. Let's go have lunch!"

The hand let go of the knob, and the voices began to fade as they walked away.

Colin and Seraphina exhaled.

Seraphina stuck her head out into the room. The coast looked clear. She yanked the toy out of Colin's hand and threw it back into the box.

"Come on," she motioned him out of the storage closet and held her finger up to her mouth again for good measure.

"Easy, turbo," she cautioned as they moved the plant slowly down the hallway into the room with the fuse box. "Right there. Good. OK, you know what to do now, right?"

Colin nodded, and they each set out on their way, tiptoeing down the hallway.

In fact, they got a good deal longer than thirty minutes' worth of eavesdropping. The office manager had panicked, canceled the rest of the patients for the day, and the staff enjoyed a good long lunch before everyone went home. Colin and Seraphina each got an earful of all *sorts* of gossip—some of which they each felt sure would help Dewey at least get headed in the right direction.

The next day, Seraphina, Colin, and Dewey sat in the living room at Colin's dad's apartment debriefing.

"Narwhalians, did you know that Laila's sister's ex-husband is in jail? And that they think that he might be the Parkside Strangler?!" reported Colin. "And that someone named Terry is really mad at someone named Anne because Anne always gets away with coming to work, like, ten minutes late every day, and Dr. Bernard never does anything about it?"

"Colin! What did you hear to help Dewey?" blurted out Seraphina.

"Oh, that. Sure. Well, they are all upset that Dewey's dad is leaving. They think that it's because Dr. Bernard takes Dewey's dad's share of the money or something. I didn't totally understand. It's like Dewey's dad has to give him some of his patient money? Or Dewey's dad has to give him some percent or something."

"That's good, Colin. That's really good."

Colin nodded and smiled a toothless smile. He was playing it cool, but inside he felt really proud that he could somehow help Dewey.

"Seraphina?"

"Actually, I didn't get much from them talking to one another. Dr. Bernard said since his day was cancelled he was heading out to play tennis and left. But your dad spoke on the phone for a while, and I did catch one side of his conversation.

"I couldn't figure out who he was talking to though—someone named Susie, I think?"

"Oh, yeah, that's my aunt Susie, his sister," explained Dewey.

"Well, he was telling her how excited he is about Alaska. He went on about the great schools and the adventure and how it would be something that would be . . . 'exciting.' I think he used that word a couple of times.

"From what I could tell, she seemed to be asking how you guys, you and your family, felt, because he talked about you guys not being as excited, and then he said something I didn't get about—wait, I wrote it down—'Oh, that ol' dream.'

"I have no idea what that meant, but I wrote

it down because it must have meant something, even though he just said that it was dumb. Maybe it might help."

"Thanks, you guys. That's pretty good. You shut down the power, eh? My dad was all mad about his day being canceled!"

"It's all I could come up with! Don't ever tell him it was me, OK? Promise, Dewey?"

"Ha! I'm pretty sure we're all in this together. Pass the cheese puffs, my toothless friend. To friendship," Dewey raised a cheese puff in the air.

Horsefeathers

The next day when Clara slid in, she found Dewey on the floor of his office with little pieces of paper all over the floor, cut out and placed here and there, trying to piece together what it all meant. He was trying to piece together what he should do.

Wolfie made high-pitched little half-barking sounds in his sleep that made him sound part bird and part dolphin—*Chirrup, click, click.*

"Boss," said Clara. "Dewey," she sighed. "Come sit down with me," she scooted over

Wolfie, who was dreaming about catching squirrels.

"May I make a suggestion?"

She continued on without giving him to a chance to reply.

"Ask your parents what's going on. Tell them you heard them talking and that you're upset. Just talk to them."

"Really?" asked Dewey. The idea of just asking them about it had not really occurred to him, in part because he'd felt like he wasn't even supposed to know about the move yet.

"But I'm not even supposed to know about us moving," he objected.

"Do you?"

"What?"

"Know about them moving?"

"Clara!"

"Well, then the rest of this is just horsefeathers."

"Ha!" laughed Dewey. "Horsefeathers is a

funny word! I rather prefer 'balderdash' myself," he said, putting on airs.

"Hogwash, hooey-balooey, claptrap, poppycock, applesauce, flimflam! Call it what you want, Dewey Fairchild. You need to sit down with your parents and have a heart-to-heart! Sir," she added, her crow's feet smiling. It was clear who was the real boss at the moment.

"Hmmm," said Dewey. "Hmmm."

That night at dinner, Dewey hung around in the kitchen longer than usual while his dad did the dishes.

"Dad? Can I talk to you?"

"Sure. Can you dry and talk at the same time?"

"Uugh. I'm tired. I've been on my feet all day," complained Dewey.

"Oh, yeah. Right. I forgot. We dentist types sit all day. You're right, son. Sit down and rest.

Your mom and I will work, cook, and do all the cleaning."

Uh oh. This wasn't getting off to a very good start.

"Dad, I'll do them tomorrow. Deal?"

"Hmm, OK. Deal. But I'm holding you to that. So what's on your mind?"

"Moving," Dewey surprised even himself by just blurting it out. He seemed to be doing a lot of that lately.

"Oh. Ha! I guess your mom and I aren't quite as stealthy as we think we are, huh?"

"I guess not," said Dewey.

His dad stopped doing the dishes, dried his hands on the towel, and sat down at the table.

And then there came the requisite talk about how much he thought the family would love Alaska. All of the many virtues of a life in Alaska. Imagine an Eskimo Boy Scout troop in Alaska. The Aurora Borealis! The annual Moose Droppings Festival. That kind of thing.

But then, Dewey asked, "But why, Dad. Can you tell me *why?*"

And his dad surprised him and said something that actually mattered.

"You know, son, as long as I can remember, I've wanted to run my own business. And this is my opportunity to do just that. Dr. Bernard is offering me the chance to open up a practice in Alaska that he's going to front so that someday he can retire there. It's mine to run, though. I get to make all the decisions—set things up my way."

"But don't you do that now?" asked Dewey.

"No. Not really. It's Dr. Bernard's business. I just work for him. He took me on fifteen years ago, and, frankly, by now I expected that we'd be partners. But it's not moving that direction. And I don't want to keep working for another person, even one whom I respect as much as Dr. Bernard. Do you understand, Dewey?"

Dewey thought he did. He liked being his own boss too, and he was only eleven. He figured by his dad's age you'd probably get sick of someone else telling you what to do all the time.

But Alaska? Surely there'd be a way out of this now that he knew the problem, though it seemed more complicated than ever.

"I see," said Dewey before nodding. "Dad. I can finish the dishes now. My feet got to rest while we were talking."

Dewey's dad patted him on the head. "You're a good boy. We'll make your sisters do them tomorrow then." He left the room with his mind already on other dad things, like how he was going to find time to wash the car tomorrow and where, since his favorite place was closed for remodeling.

Dewey, on the other hand, was not done with this topic. He finished washing the dishes and set his mind to following up the conversation with his mother. First he needed to think. He knew she didn't want to go either, but he had to come up with some way to get her to understand that they needed Dad to be happy doing what he does here. And fast.

⬭

Unfortunately for Dewey, he didn't get that time to think to himself because his father told his mother about their conversation, and she sprang it on him in his least favorite way.

"Dewey, I have some things I'd like to talk with you about," she said as she sat at the end of his bed with *The Three Musketeers,* evidently nothing more than a tease this evening, in her lap.

No matter how she said those words, be they gently, friendly, kindly, warmly, casually, or calmly, they *always* sent Dewey into a small panic. *Oh, no! What does she want now? What did I do?*

This time, it was about his conversation with his dad, and he was totally unprepared for that. He hadn't expected his dad would have spoken to her this quickly. He hadn't had time to plot, strategize, or plan at all.

"Dad says you have some questions and concerns about us moving to Alaska."

"No," he said unprepared for the lump that landed in his throat and the tears that started to well up in his eyes. "I just don't want to go, that's all."

"Oh," she said gently, smiling warmly as she picked him up off the pillow to hug him, letting the book slip down between them. "Is that all?"

He buried his face in her shoulder but didn't let himself really cry.

He sat up, and she wiped his cheek even though no tears had come out.

"Did you know Dad doesn't like his job?" asked Dewey.

"Did he tell you that?"

"Not exactly. But he said he wants to go to Alaska so he can be his own boss."

"Oh. Yes, I see. Well, that's true. I think there

is some truth to that. I also think he likes an adventure. But you know what I mostly think?" she continued. "I think these are very grown up decisions, and you can trust us to make good ones for the family."

"But I don't want to move to Alaska! I have friends here! A life! Stephanie has a life! Pooh Bear, well, not so much, but *we* do. I have a career of my own, you know!"

"Oh, you do, do you?"

"Oh, you wouldn't understand. I'm just saying, I don't want to start over."

"And I'm just saying, I don't really want to start over either. And if you've heard we're moving, why then, I guess you've heard that much as well. But you're going to have to leave it to us to make the decisions about what's best for the family."

Dewey sighed. "OK, Mom."

"Do you want me to read to you, still?"

"OK," he said, sounding a bit defeated. But

he was finding it very hard to concentrate, so he soon feigned exhaustion and asked her to turn out the light.

"Mom?" he asked as she was closing his door, "is the crust on bread really healthier for you?"

"It is."

"Why?"

She walked back to the side of his bed and kissed his forehead. "More antioxidants. Night, Dewey."

Hmm. More antioxidants. Go figure. Good to know.

Big News

Standing under the vent in his room, Dewey could hear the hushed whispers of his parents.

"I told you that the kids would catch on, and we should have told them ourselves."

"Yes, you're probably right," she sighed. "But I want to talk about something Dewey mentioned that you told him."

"What's that?"

"Why are we going to Alaska, again?" his mother asked.

"My father always said, Karen, never ask a

question when you already know the answer."

"Don!"

"Well, come on, Karen. We've been through this. Bernard has told me he doesn't really have as much business for me here and needs me to relocate to Alaska."

"But you told Dewey more . . . about being your own boss and how much that means to you."

"Aw, come on, Karen. Can't a father and son have a little sit down and dream time? Sure. Yes. That's what I said."

"I'm not saying there's anything wrong with that."

CRASH! Dewey, who had been stretching up as high as he could toward the vent so as to not miss a single word, fell off of the nightstand he was standing on. The drawer had opened up and spilled out, tipping over the nightstand and making a horribly loud crash.

For Pete's sake! Thinking fast, he pulled a

framed painting from kindergarten off the wall and threw it on the floor. Its glass shattered, and he dove back into bed, shoving his nightstand back into place as he scrambled.

His parents came rushing in his room. "What happened?!" they asked. His sisters padded their way sleepily down the hallway to see what all the noise was about.

"I think the nail must have come out of the wall," claimed Dewey, feigning sleepiness and shock.

By the time his parents cleaned it all up, they all went to bed much later than was good for anybody, and if Dewey's parents' conversation continued that night, he wasn't privy to it.

Still, something other than that dresser had given way beneath him. Dewey couldn't explain it yet, but he felt some shifting inside of him, an unsteady, but promising "titch" of hope.

"¡Seraphina! Por favor. ¡Chicle en la basura!" Seraphina got up and dropped her gum in the trash and shot a smile at Dewey. Dewey had caught her up on all he knew at recess, and she had passed him a note about five minutes ago. They'd already relied once on the kindness of neighbors to help them pass a note back and forth, and this presented one more opportunity to deliver a message.

> Seraphina: Did you ever find out what your Aunt's comment meant?
>
> Dewey: No.
>
> D: Need to . . . I should call her tonight.
>
> S: Email her! Tell her it's a school project or something . . . need to write a story about your parents when they were kids.
>
> D: OK. Save this paper for your gum next time! Place gum here

He drew a neat little circle for her to place her gum.

To: Auntie Susie

Subject: My Dad!

Hi, Auntie Susie!

How are you? I have to write a paper for school about my parents when they were kids. Can you tell me:

- a couple funny things Dad used to do
- a couple things he used to do that made you mad
- something he got in trouble for once
- any dreams or wishes he used to have for himself
- anything else you think I should know?

Thanks! Say hi to Uncle Eddie.

Sincerely Yours,

Dewey

Among other things, Dewey learned that his dad had taken the family car and driven it downtown when he was just a few years older than Dewey! And his dad could also, it seems, play entire symphonies of hand farts.

He definitely planned to make good use of these golden nuggets one day soon. But right now, the most valuable and, frankly, shocking piece of information his aunt had revealed was that his dad's dream had always been to be a high school math teacher.

Now, Dewey wasn't exactly a numbers man, and this information made zero sense to him. A math teacher? He'd never once heard his dad say *anything* about teaching of any kind. This just seemed weird and totally out of nowhere.

But his aunt's email left little room for doubt.

As long as I've known your dad he always wanted to be a teacher. When I was a kid he used to make me pretend to be one of his students. He'd call roll and make me say "here!" He used to torture me and make me do homework with him. I hated it; he'll tell you that! But he loved it. And he loved math. I think that's why dental school came so easily to him. Math being the language of science and all. And my parents just couldn't see a man being a high school teacher. Isn't that awful! It was law school, dental school, medical school, or business. I don't think he ever really saw it as an option. Well, dear, just cut and paste! I think I've gone on and on so much I've written an essay for you!

When he brought this information back to Clara, she did it *again,* and Dewey started to feel downright exasperated with her.

"You know what to do," she declared. "Back to your parents with this information, Dewey. Lickety-split."

"What! How would I possibly explain to them how I know any of this! No way, Clara. Uh uh. Not gonna do it. Come up with another plan."

But Clara insisted that time was running out, and he needed to work with them directly.

To his annoyance, Seraphina agreed with Clara, and, as in the case with Michael and his mother, had her own spin to put on the plan.

"Why don't you tell your dad that you're writing an article for school about moving to

Alaska? Tell him you'll be interviewing him and people he knows. You know like a 'One man's journey with his family to Alaska.' That way you can explain why you sought out the info. In fact, why *don't* you actually write a piece for the school paper? Colin writes for *The Crest*. Ask him."

"Why would the school paper want a piece on us moving to Alaska?" asked Dewey incredulously, though he did like the idea of at least having an alibi for why he had the information.

Clara approved. Wolfie too. Dewey was outnumbered.

But boy, oh boy. Dewey still felt really confused about his dad wanting to be a math teacher in his past life. He felt more interested in that than why they were going to Alaska, frankly. It was just so weird. And so was the expression Clara had just used—lickety-split. Lickety-split. Lickety-split. It sounded like a train heading down the tracks. Maybe he'd just muse over the origins of lickety-split for a while and not move quite so lickety-split-ish.

Captain Obvious

The spring semester was breezing by, and there didn't seem to be much talk about the move these days.

Dewey never could bring himself to do that school paper interview of his dad or ask him any more questions about what he had discovered. He was deep into a science project at school. He'd also been busy, of course, at work, because where you found kids, you always found parents who needed some assistance to be, shall we say, their best selves.

For his project, Dewey wanted to look at what burned more quickly: 91% isopropyl rubbing alcohol, the petroleum hydrocarbon Tiki Torch fuel they used to fill the Tiki torches in the yard when they had company, or tequila.

His teacher had done a whole two days on fire safety first, but try to tell his mother that.

"Dewey, I'm telling you. I don't care what Mr. Stewart says. I'm not having you run experiments with blowing things up at home."

"I'll go outside," shrugged Dewey.

"Thank you. I *much* prefer our house to burn from the outside in. No," she remained adamant, an afghan draped around her shoulders.

"But, Mom," Dewey pleaded. "It's my project. I've done all the research and steps leading up to it already."

She pushed her hair out of her face. "Do you like my eyebrows, Dewey?"

"What?" *That seemed random*, Dewey thought.

"My eyebrows?" she asked, refocusing him

back on what she said. "Look at them. *Do you like my eyebrows?*" Each word was enunciated clearly like he was a foreign exchange student.

"Sure. I guess so. Yeah." Truthfully, he'd never even really thought about the fact that she even had eyebrows, but they looked fine to him.

"I like yours, too. And I don't really want you walking around without any because you singed them while flambéing our lawn chair."

Just then Dewey's dad came in.

"Dad. Help!"

"Karen. It'll be fine. Dewey and I will do it on the driveway in the front. Don't worry!"

"Uugh! Don't leave burn stains on my driveway!" she called out after his dad, who headed out the door, one arm around Dewey's shoulder and the other reaching for the bottle of tequila.

"This is all a cover for your father to have a margarita party in the driveway," laughed his mom to Stephanie, who'd been sitting at the table trying to drown everyone out as she did her homework.

"Save me a taco," Stephanie mumbled.

"I wuant a taco!" called out Pooh Bear from the other room.

"Ha! I know what we're doing for dinner tonight," laughed their mom. "They better not blow something up. I'm going to *kill* them if they kill themselves."

The next day Dewey was working on some of his predictions and trying to graph them on his computer when his mom dropped a small package on his desk.

"You got a letter from Auntie Susie," she said.

She hung around waiting for him to open it. He stopped what he was doing, eager to tear open the small package, but he worried about what she might see.

"Well, aren't you going to open it?" she asked.

"Sure. Yeah," he could see no way to stall.

Dear Dewey,

I hope this isn't too late for your school project. This is a diary from your dad when he was about your age. I probably should hand it over to him, not you, but what the heck—you're my only nephew, and we'll call this sweet revenge for all the times he tortured me!

Please do take care of it, though, as I would like it to get back me in good shape when you're done. Someday, I plan to torture him myself with it and read parts of it aloud—like at his fiftieth birthday party.

Hugs and Kisses,
Auntie Susie

"Wow," said his mom. "Let me see that!"

"Hey! She sent it to me."

"But this is quite an artifact. What project? How about we read it together tonight at bedtime?"

"OK," agreed Dewey. "It's not really a project. It's nothing. I was going to maybe write an article about our family going to Alaska for the school paper, and I sent Auntie Susie some interview questions about Dad as a kid. I don't really think the school paper gives a rat's behind about Dad taking us to Alaska."

"Really?" asked Dewey's mom. "I would think that might make a great feature piece."

"Yeah, maybe," Dewey said just to move the subject along.

No one cared and Dewey didn't care to think about it anymore. He'd just cured Alexander Bravo's mother of her embarrassing habit of dressing like a teenager with her heart and flower tank tops, short shorts, and leather boots. Now *that* was something to write home about.

When his mom left the room, Dewey went back to his science project. But as he entered his data into the computer, his mind kept wandering back to the diary on the desk next to him. He picked it up and opened it up randomly to a page and began to read. He flipped around and read another and another.

He couldn't believe it. It was *the* most boring drivel he'd ever read. Incredibly, each page read the same. School was fine. His dad hoped he didn't have to run in PE. He didn't like a girl named Dee Dee. He did like a girl named Dee Dee. No, he didn't. Yes, he did. He had to run in PE.

At the end of each entry he ranked the day. "All in all today was a 'B'."

> *July 4: It is the fourth of July. The Blatts and Joneses came over. It was fun. We swam all day and ate a lot.*

There's not very much else to say. All in all, today was a B+.

Seriously? He wrote on the entry for July fourth, 'It is the fourth of July'? Ha! Thank you, Captain Obvious!

September 6: Today I worked in Pop's office. It was boring. Then I got my hair cut. It really doesn't show. Four more days until school starts. Uugh. I got into Drama Honors and I didn't even have to try out because the class wasn't full. All in all, today was a "C." P.S. Anthony (my dog) really likes to lick ear wax.

Dewey flipped through looking for the "A" days and, frankly, they were so dull, he thought he'd put a bullet through his head.

Wow. Could his father have led such a dull existence?

Maybe he was just a poor recorder of history.

When his mom tried to read it to him that evening she laughed, and they both agreed Alexander Dumas's *The Three Musketeers* made better reading than Don Fairchild's "One Musketeer," and they moved on.

Still, after his mother left, Dewey got to thinking again. His aunt had said his dad had wanted to be a math teacher. And clearly, he was one bored kid in school. There had to be something Dewey had not uncovered yet. What could it be?

That night, Dewey had a dream that he and his dad were going on a vacation together. They were going to take a jeep ride, but first they had to go over this huge big bump that he worried the jeep couldn't handle. Then it would be smooth sailing.

The jeep went over the bump fine, he guessed, because the dream just skipped to another part, and they were now driving along the water's edge. It was beautiful, but Dewey worried they might fall into the water in the dream, so he asked his dad to open a window so they could swim out if the jeep fell in.

As they were driving along, he realized that they'd taken these trips before. He loved taking them with his dad and how they traveled together on the open road. In his dream they were driving together and Dewey felt happy—because they were together.

When he woke up, darkness filled his room, but the light of the moon seeped through the sides of his blackout shades. He wrote the dream down by turning on his phone and emailing the details of it to himself, so he wouldn't forget it in the morning.

"I've got it," he said aloud to the moonlit darkness. "I know the solution."

Tiny Developments

Every year since Dewey began preschool, they'd driven the same route to school past one set of deciduous trees.

The west coast of the country doesn't really have seasons in the way the rest of the country does, but he and his mom could track them by this one stretch of tree-lined houses where the leaves would, like clockwork, start to turn colors at the start of school, begin to fall at Halloween, go barren for winter, and bring green little buds of new growth in the spring.

The trees stayed the same height, but Dewey grew and grew each year, and this year, when the little green buds of spring came to life, Dewey Fairchild had grown enough to help solve his own father's problem.

Dewey's dad was bored, and he needed a change.

Dewey may have been gifted in his field—an accomplished parent problem solver—but it was Clara who helped him understand kids are not meant to parent their *own* parents.

"Dewey, my boy. Sir. You've done marvelous work here. You cracked the case. Now, it's time for Wolfie and me to step in."

"What do you mean?"

"I mean, I'm in charge now. Coffee break time. Take a load off. Take ten. Sabbatical. Shore leave. Go put your feet up."

"Shore leave?" Dewey laughed. "OK. See what you guys can do. My fate is in your hands. And my teeth are in your cookies. I'm starving."

With that, he prepared to work on some other clients' cases and eat some lemon basil cookies.

"No, no, noo," she said, packing up his cookies in a little to-go pack. "Off you go. I don't want to see hide nor hair of you for a week."

Wolfie was nudging him along toward the door with his nose.

"What? Really? You're serious?"

"As a heart attack. Now go. Do something enjoyable. Read a good book. Knit. Build a model plane. Paint a masterpiece. Write a novel. Plant a—"

"OK, OK. I get the idea!"

"Wait. One message. Georgina called. Allergies. And acid reflux. Her father's on the road to health. Just thought you'd want to know."

"Yeah. That's good news," he replied distractedly. Truthfully, he could hardly take it in. He hadn't expected this development regarding his own business with Clara. But she looked like she meant business. Exhausted from staying up late, he was all too pleased to go off and do nothing but munch cookies, play some games with Colin on his computer, and not try to fix anyone or anything for a while.

Seraphina paced back and forth in her room. She hadn't heard anything from Dewey in quite some time, and, really, she couldn't think of anything she felt like doing.

She sent him a text but got no reply. He didn't always have his phone with him so that might not mean anything. They weren't at an age where they carried them around like older kids did.

She'd have to wait to run into him at lunch or pass him a note in Spanish.

Seraphina liked to collect rocks, and she pulled out her collection to see if she could organize the ones already on her dresser by color gradation today.

She had her basic igneous, sedimentary, and

metamorphic categories of rocks and liked to move them around sometimes based on size and texture and other times by their color.

Her phone buzzed on her desk and the vibration of it against the wood laminate startled her and made her jump.

She saw a picture of Dewey with her house address numbers behind him.

Confused, she just sat looking at it.

Then he texted:

Knock, knock!

Oh! He was at her front door!

Coming!

She texted back and ran down to open the door for him.

"Hi! Come in," she said, and she stepped back, realizing that he wasn't alone but was petting a rather large dog on her porch.

"Yours, I assume?" he said.

"No!" she replied with surprise as she leaned over to pet the friendly beast as well.

His—or was it her?—fur was apricot colored with a white chest. The dog probably stood as tall as a yardstick in Seraphina's estimation. She'd never seen such a large dog!

"Where did you find her?"

Dewey peered under the large, 200-pound dog's frame. "Um, I'm going with him."

"Ha! Great, Dewey. Good to know. OK then. Where did you find *him*?"

"Right here. On your porch. That's why I thought he was yours."

"Well, I can assure you he's not. There's no way in—" At that moment, the dog shook his massive head and drool flew all over Dewey and Seraphina.

"Ewww!" They both exclaimed.

Seraphina regretted it afterwards, though, because the dog looked big and sweet and friendly about it all.

"Hang on. I'll be back with a towel!"

When she came back out, she found the dog sitting at Dewey's feet.

"Does he have a collar?" she asked as she wiped herself off and handed Dewey the now slightly damp towel.

"Gee, thanks," he said, trying to find a dry spot to use. "No. No collar. He sure is big and friendly, though."

"Yeah, he's kind of sweet," she said, staying clear of his head in case he got any big ideas again. She petted the bottom half of his body.

"Here," she said to Dewey as she passed him one of Bigboy's doggie treats. "Give him one of these."

The treats were about the size of a corn-flake and this dog's tongue was about the size of Bigboy! He took the treat, but didn't even seem to notice it was there.

"Give me those!" said Dewey, and he poured the entire bag of them into the dog's mouth.

The dog chewed twice, gulped, and looked up with his eyes asking for more.

"Sorry, little guy, that's all we've got," said Dewey.

"Maybe we should walk around with him and see if anyone's lost him."

"That's pretty funny, Seraphina. He's a pretty big dog to lose, don't you think?"

"Well, somebody obviously lost him. And he can't just stay here!"

"Why don't we take a picture of him and print out some signs?" suggested Dewey. "That might be easier than trying to figure out how to haul him around the neighborhood."

"Good idea. Do you think we can just leave him alone out here?"

"Sure. I found him that way."

As soon as they went inside though, the large dog began to whine and cry. And then he heaved up his big body and jumped up on the screen door.

"Oh no! Get him down!" cried Seraphina. "He's going to break the door."

"Better bring him in with us," reasoned Dewey.

"Oh boy. Oh boy. OK."

The mastiff followed them in, and despite Seraphina's concerns, did not swallow the flat screen TV or the dining room table and just settled down again at their feet while they worked. They searched online until they found dogs that looked like him and concluded he must be a mastiff.

> Found: Apricot Big Dog. Looks like a Mastiff (?) located near Anvil Drive, male. Please call or text 555-555-2222

Seraphina's parents wouldn't want her plastering her address all over the place, but this should work fine. They took the pooch's picture, and they were just printing out the last signs when Seraphina's mom came into the room.

"Oh! I see you've met Peewee!"

Seraphina's face was blank as she tried to grasp the meaning of this development from her mother. Her mother knew this dog?

"I need to put this collar on him. Come here, Peewee," Seraphina's mother said and proceeded to put a collar the size of one of Seraphina's dad's belts around the dog's neck.

"Seraphina, Peewee. Peewee, Seraphina. Dewey, this is Seraphina's new dog, Peewee. He's charmed to meet you, I'm sure. I'll be back in thirty minutes," she called out over her shoulder. "He eats like eight cups of food a day. I need to go get some more. The shelter only gave us one meal's worth to get us started."

"Whoa," uttered Seraphina.

"Whoa," repeated Dewey. "That's a really big lap dog you got there, Seraphina."

"Yeah," said Seraphina, still too dazed to really believe that this small drooling horse was all hers for the snuggling.

"Um, well, Peewee, it looks like you're no longer lost. You've been found," she said a bit tentatively and pet him on the head, also a bit tentatively.

She noted gratefully that he didn't always seem to shake his head in response. OK then, one thing at a time. Maybe she could grow a bigger lap.

Bringing it Home

Just like that, life had a way of offering the unexpected. Dewey, an average boy, who was averagely average, became one of the most sought after kids in town, Seraphina was now the proud owner of a dog the size of Canada, and Dewey and his family were moving to Alaska.

And then, just like that, just like that moment when the first little underarm hair pops out—and you think *where the fruit did that come from?!*— Dewey's dad announced they weren't moving, after all.

Dewey and his family all sat around the table Sunday evening. Dewey's mom took away the ketchup bottle as Dewey drowned his fries in ketchup.

"Aw, come on, Mom," objected Dewey.

"Dr. Jay says children under the age of eighteen shouldn't be allowed to operate heavy ketchup or syrup bottles."

"Hmph," said Dewey, but he smiled. He loved his pediatrician.

His dad clinked his glass with his fork and spoke, "Gang, I have some big news. The plans have changed, and it's big. I'm going to need everyone's support. I'm quitting my job. I've given this a lot of thought.

"I don't want to be a dentist. The good news is you don't have to go to Alaska. The tougher news is I'm going back to school, and we're all going to have to pitch in a bit for me to do so."

That wasn't "tougher" news. The resounding cheers and applause heard round the table, and the world, from that one little family could have powered an army to victory.

Their father felt humbled both by how much they obviously had not wanted to go, and also by their support, and he began to tear up. He put down his fork. So did Dewey and the others, except Pooh Bear who was working very diligently on attaching a pea to each prong of hers.

"I've always wanted to teach math. It's been in my heart and been my passion. No one ever told me I could. I just didn't ever consider it a real choice that I could make."

Dewey's mother went over to her husband and gave him a long kiss on the cheek and hugged him around the back of his shoulders.

"What made you change your mind?" she asked.

"You know," he said, "I can't really go into it right now."

Dewey could have sworn right then that he caught his father shoot the slightest glance his way—and that he saw traces of cookie crumbs on his chin.

"But I'll say this much. I was never a very happy kid in school. And I think I can be a much better teacher to kids than the teachers I had growing up. I think I can make it enjoyable and applicable. Who knows? Maybe we'll even blow some things up while we're at it."

Say, this gave Dewey an idea. His dad wasn't the only one miserable in school. Curing parents' problems might just be the beginning. Maybe next year he'd start branching out. He had a feeling the kids might be lining up for him to cure their teacher problems!

"Does this mean I don't have to help Dewey with his math anymore?" asked Stephanie.

"Oh, sure," replied Dewey. "If you call sitting on me building my math skills, then you've been amazing."

Everyone laughed and Mom patted Dewey on the head.

They weren't going to Alaska. He group texted Seraphina and Colin: Best news, ever! Not moving to Alaska!!!!!!! It felt so good to have friends.

Just what, he wondered, had Clara said and done to bring it all, well, *home*?

He looked over at his dad and smiled. "I'm glad we're not going to Alaska, Dad. All in all, I think this has been an A+ day."

ABOUT THE AUTHOR

Lorri Horn, born and raised in California, has been working with kids all her life. She got her first babysitting job when she was nine years old, became a camp counselor, and went on to be a teacher. It's true she did eat all of the pickles and popsicles on her first babysitting gig, but she did manage to feed that kid a cheese and pickle sandwich before polishing off the rest of the jar herself. No one complained. Evidently, she had a knack with kids.

Lorri spent a few years studying cercopithecus aethiops (vervet monkeys) and thought she'd be a famous biological anthropologist. But it turns out you have to rough it and camp to do that kind of job, and Lorri's more of a pillow-top mattress and no bug-repellent kind of gal. Plus, while it was fascinating to study and observe our little non-human primate brothers and sisters lip-smacking to communicate things like "Oh, gee, I'm sorry, is that your branch?", Lorri found it much more rewarding to share a good book with a kid. Not once did those vervets gather round for story-time.

So Lorri became an educator and an author for humans, who, admittedly, sometimes monkey around. She has a degree in English, a teaching credential, has been Nationally Board Certified, and has taught public school for over 14 years. She loves cheese (if she had to choose between cheese and chocolate on a deserted island, she'd have to say cheese—and that's saying a whole lot, because she's not sure how'd she live without chocolate), humor, baking, books, and spending time with her husband, son, and their dog—you guessed it—Wolfie.